First published in Great Britain in 2012 by Comma Press.
www.commapress.co.uk
Copyright © in the name of the individual contributor
This collection copyright © Comma Press 2012.

ISBN-13   978 1905583515

The publisher gratefully acknowledges the assistance of
Literature Northwest and Arts Council England across all its projects.

LOTTERY FUNDED
literaturenorthwest

Set in Bembo 11/13 by David Eckersall.
Printed and bound in England by MPG Biddles Ltd.

2012

THE BBC INTERNATIONAL SHORT STORY AWARD

Contents

Introduction

THE AMERICAN AUTHOR Mark Twain is often credited with the notion that it takes longer to write a short letter than a long one. Wrongly, perhaps, as the French mathematician Blaise Pascal had expressed the same thought in his correspondence several centuries before. Either way, you can see the point. Brevity, as someone else put it, is the soul of wit. But applied to works of fiction, this might suggest that a three volume novel or an epic three generation family saga is little more than a short story the author had not taken the trouble to express more succinctly. *Paradise Lost* might be better rendered as a haiku.

I am getting carried away, but chairing the judging panel for this year's BBC International Short Story Award was a perfect reminder of just how rewarding the short story genre can be. Eight thousand words – our limit – can be enough to tell a tale that lingers as long in the mind as many a work of much greater length.

For this year only, the year of the London Olympics, the Award has gone international. Entries were invited from anywhere in the world and the judges were asked to identify a shortlist of ten, instead of the usual five. Appropriately enough for a short story competition, this Award's shortlist is particularly important – very nearly as important as the decision on the winner and runner-up – as being selected for the shortlist secures not only a place in this anthology, but also a broadcast on BBC Radio 4.

It turns out that short story writing is indeed an international phenomenon. Entries came from all round the world. On the judging panel we considered more than 70 from over 500 eligible entries, but even when they were reduced to our final ten they proved to be a global mix, with stories set in Britain, Ireland, the Balkans, North America, Australia, Africa and Asia.

Covered were such universal human activities as homicide, adultery, drunkenness, invention, inspiration and even levitation. In addition to the human dramas, there are more than mere walk-on parts for a goose, a dog and a brand-new brand of vodka. A river runs through two of our stories; some tales are played out in front of a backcloth of ancient feuds; in others, central to the plot is modern technology.

The shortness of the story does not have to limit the wideness of its scope. In this volume we have small incidents examined minutely, but also whole lives painted in some detail on a miniature canvas. Many express real, raw emotion; one or two take the reader into the surreal and absurd. Throughout, there is to be found love and loss and laughs, not a little sadness and even a touch, here and there, of pornography. And quite often, at the end, a surprise.

To orchestrate the decision-making process, I was put in charge of an impressive band of expert judges appointed to analyse, criticise and appreciate the entries: two precociously talented young writers – Anjali Joseph and Ross Raisin – both of whom have recently published their second novels and are already recognised by a number of literary awards; Michèle Roberts is a distinguished literary figure in two languages. A Fellow of the Royal Society of Literature, she is also a Chevalier de l'Ordre des Arts et des Lettres. In addition she is Emeritus Professor of Creative Writing at the University of East Anglia and the author of several novels, poems and short stories; Di Speirs is Editor of Readings for BBC Radio, responsible for selecting and broadcasting works of literature on BBC Radio 3 and 4, and a driving force behind this Award since its inception seven years ago.

With a varied group of judges, and an even more varied selection of stories to consider, achieving a consensus was unlikely to be straightforward, and so it proved. But the closer we got to the finishing line, the more the strengths and weaknesses of each piece of writing became apparent. And so with relatively few cuts and bruises, only a couple of false starts and no tripping or gouging, we decided which entries were to survive the heats to earn a place in the final ten, and ultimately which competitor would make it onto the winning rostrum.

To win, or to come even close to winning, a story had to survive a meticulous examination of its author's writing style and use of language. But more than that, it had to move or amuse, startle or inspire the reader in one way or another, and to continue to do so after more than one reading. In their different ways – *very* different ways – we think all ten stories achieve this, as of course did some of the others unlucky enough to be squeezed out of the running on the final lap.

But at the last there can only be one winner. Though there is the consolation of a prize for the runner-up, judged to have been just pipped at the post.

If I can use one more sporting term, it is a well-worn cliché in reporting an exciting and skilfully played match to say, no matter which team actually scored the most goals, 'football is the winner.' So whatever your view of the final result, I hope you will agree, in this competition, short story writing is the winner.

Clive Anderson

Escape Routes

Lucy Caldwell

Belfast, 1995

FOR MOST OF that year, you are obsessed with slipways and secret ways through *Zork*. Not cheats, which suddenly give you the treasures without your having to earn them: they're something else entirely. What you mean – what Christopher calls them – is wormholes. Places where it looks like you're stuck, and then squirm through to safety, whisked through space and time.

The first, and best, is in the Altar room:

```
In one corner
```

it says,

```
is a small black hole which leads to
darkness. You haven't a prayer of
getting the coffin down there.
```

For weeks, you've tried to find another way back, discarding all of your hard-won items as you go: the nasty knife, the garlic, the bottle of water, even the jewelled egg, because the voice keeps on saying that you're carrying too much. You've run through the verbs you know, and looked up others. Push coffin! Squeeze coffin! Shrink! Dismantle! Coerce! but none of them works. Then one night Christopher tells you the wormhole is 'Pray'. You blink at him.

Type it, he says, stringing his hair behind his ears. Go on. Type 'pray'.

You type it: and then, next thing, you're back in the forest, coffin and all.

You see? he says, and when you say, How did you know? he just shrugs and smiles.

Christopher's not like the other babysitters. They like to get you and your brother off to bed as soon as possible, so they can eat their pizza and watch TV and phone their friends. You listen in, sometimes, on the extension in your parents' room, the handset tilted away from your face, the mouthpiece muffled. Their conversations follow the same, set patterns; over and over and on and on, and mostly you get bored before they finish. But it's never boring when Christopher's over. When he babysits he brings floppy disks of games, *Kix* and *Deathstar*, *Repton*, *Bonecruncher*, *Labyrinth* and *Snapper*, a different selection each time, and he sits on the floor with you beside the BBC computer and tells you when to duck and where to go and what to avoid, and when the Deathstar's coming he takes over while you hide your eyes. *Zork*, which is your best game, he gave to you for your tenth birthday, for you to play whenever you wanted. He told your parents it's a series of verbal reasoning and logical puzzles, and because of this they let you play it almost as much as you want, instead of limiting it to twenty minutes after your homework and piano practice is done.

By the entrance to Hades and the desolation, where the voices lament and the evil spirits jeer – the next place you get stuck – you try Christopher's wormhole again.

```
>Pray
```

you command.

```
If you pray hard enough, your prayers
might be answered.
```

Your heart leaps.

```
>Pray hard
```

you try.

```
I don't know the word 'hard'.
```

So again you try 'pray', and 'pray', and 'pray pray pray', and 'pray the Lord's Prayer' and 'pray with all my heart'. But it doesn't work this time. Then you try typing 'pray' repeatedly, over forty-one times, you count, until your fingers are in spasms and the screen no longer seems to be moving. But the wormhole is closed, and even the thesaurus – adjure! beseech! implore! solicit! – is no good. The next time you see him, you tell Christopher about this and he says suddenly, Do you believe in prayer?

You don't know what he means, and he says, In life.

We pray in school, you say. At the end of Assembly, the Lord's Prayer, every morning.

Do you believe in it, he says. In God.

No, you say. I don't know. Maybe. Your mum and dad are atheists, which is unusual, and he knows this, and this is why he asked. You've been to church four times that you remember: for Brown Owl's wedding, and the other times for carols at Christmas. Christopher is intrigued by this. He's writing an essay, he tells you, on faith and whether it's acquired or innate. He tells you of children raised by wolves, then found by humans; he talks about men making paintings with red clay and sticks on the walls of hidden caves. You don't understand what he's saying but you listen, or pretend to, because you like Christopher, and he doesn't normally talk so much. Christopher is studying Philosophy at Queen's, plays guitar and likes Japanese girls, or so he says, though his on-off girlfriend Karen has a round reddish face and limp blonde hair and isn't even remotely Japanese. You don't like Karen. Sometimes when Christopher is babysitting, she comes too, and she sits on the sofa with her magazine and expects him to sit beside her and huffs loud sighs if you ask him to help with a tricky level. She's always asking him to cut his hair too, and he never does, and she gets cross about it. He's got long hair, longer than yours, which he wears centre-parted and tucked behind his ears, tied into a ponytail at the neck, and she says it's disgusting on a man. She says to him, Even your own mother says the same, for goodness' sake. But your mum says Good on him, He's unafraid to be an individual, Instead of following the herd.

As Christopher talks, blinking and waggling his hands, you wonder what it would be like to kiss him, like Karen does, suction mouths and squashy lips. The thought of it used to gross you out. But recently it's been making you jittery, a hollow feeling in your stomach that you don't quite understand.

The summer Christopher goes missing, you only see him twice: while things are uncertain during the summer months, your parents tend not to go out. The second-last time, his mother and yours get stuck across town – a funeral, and then some kind of scare, the bridges closed – and he takes you and your brother back to his. He's looking after a puppy for a friend and his mum is worried it'll have the utility room destroyed if it's left alone too long: your mothers were only supposed to be gone for a couple of hours. The puppy is mostly miniature Schnauzer with maybe a dash of something else: it has whiskers and a fringe and a face like a little old man. It's six months old, and still too small for its paws. It's whining and crying when you get there, pressing into the gap between the tumble-drier and the wall. It takes ten minutes and a trail of doggy chocolate-buttons to entice it out, while Christopher mixes bleach in a pail and mops up its puddles. Once it's out, you pet and cuddle it like a baby, and eventually it starts to get bolder, yipping and nipping at your fingers, and then the three of you take it out into the garden for a game of chase.

After a while you need the toilet, and go inside. The house is a bungalow, with the bedrooms and guest bathroom off one long corridor. On your way back, you pause at the door of Christopher's room. It's slightly ajar, and you tell yourself that you're not spying, because the door was open anyway: and before you know it, you've slipped inside and you're standing in his bedroom. Although you've been to the house many times, you've never been inside this room. It smells musty and herbal: forbidden. The curtains are closed, even though it's daytime, but there's enough light leaking through for you to see: the rumpled unmade bed, the guitars propped up against the far wall, the balled-up socks and the shed skins of t-shirts. You take a tiny step inside, and another. Glued to the walls, and the wardrobe doors, and even covering most of the inside wardrobe mirror, are pictures of bands, and one band in particular, a band you know Christopher loves: the Manic Street Preachers. The biggest picture is ripped from a newspaper, and it shows a man with letters carved into his arm: actually carved, with angry rough slashes of a knife. You trace them out: 4 REAL, they say. There's a fluttery feeling in your stomach, a giddy, hot-sick feeling, and you are suddenly slightly breathless as you squint at the newsprint reporting that *Richey Edwards went missing on the day...*

A noise outside makes you jump, and you realise it's the back door slamming, the others coming in. You slip from the room, taking care to leave the door exactly as it was, and go back to meet them in the kitchen, your heart opening and closing in your chest like a fist.

Two weeks later, the last time you see him, Christopher promises not to tell when he finds you and Alison McKeag from down the road smoking ripped-up sachets of bouquet garni wrapped up in loo roll out of the bathroom window. He just laughs and says so long as you stick to smoking herbs you're fine, it's tobacco that's evil, and tobacco companies. Then he says, God it really stinks in here you know, but before you panic about your parents he helps to push the window open past its paint-stiff hinge, and wash the flakes down the sink, and he gets a can of Lynx from his bag to spray to hide the smell. You just say it was me, he says, if they say anything. Say I was meeting Karen afterwards and wanted to freshen up.

Are you? you ask, a bit cheekily, emboldened by the presence of Alison McKeag.

He looks at you. No, he says. She dumped me last week.

Sorry, you say, not knowing what to say, and Alison titters.

I'm going to put the pizza on, he says, after a pause that stretches too long, do you two want any?

No, says Alison. And then she says, Us two are away to talk about girly things, aren't we?

Yeah, you say, and you try to make your eyes say sorry, but Christopher just smiles and says Fair play.

Later, when Alison's gone, you find him sitting on the sofa, just sitting, the TV not even on. Your brother's oblivious, playing *Deathstar* next door, squealing and yelping along with the beeps.

Do you want to play *Zork*? you say. I've got to a new bit I'm stuck on.

Once you've booted your brother off, the two of you play for more than an hour. Christopher tells you the trick is not just to take the sceptre, but wave it, 'wave sceptre' – not a wormhole, exactly, but something you'd never have thought of – and suddenly the rainbow is solid. Not now, but later, he says, you'll need to walk over it. For the moment, he says, look around, and you 'look around', and there where there wasn't before is a pot of gold.

Hey! you say, but he just says, Southwest now, and all the way back to Canyon View. Then northwest to the Clearing, and West back to the window and into the kitchen, and west again back to the living room to put your treasures into the case.

Why are you telling me this? you ask, because normally – unless you're about to be killed – he lets you work it out for yourself.

There's three more parts, he says, and this is only Part I, although it's taken you months to work out how to make it this far.

How do you know all this anyway, you say then, annoyed.

He just shrugs, and plucks at the rubber band keeping his hair back.

Are you sad about Karen, you suddenly say, looking away from him back at the screen, and feeling your face rush hot.

Karen, he says, in a way that sounds like a no but could be a yes, and you don't know how to ask again.

Maybe you'll meet someone Japanese next time, you think of saying, but there are no Japanese people in Belfast.

So you say nothing, and just make your way through the forest again as he rocks on his heels and watches.

You finish Part I, and diligently play a week's worth of Part II, wanting to surprise him with how far you've got, drowning again and again in the maintenance room of the dam until you work out not to push the blue button, just the yellow. In the end, though, you never get further than this, because that's when he goes missing. Your parents tell you, calmly. He'll turn up, they say. He's probably with friends in Glasgow, that's what Karen's suggested, and he's got friends in Manchester too, so they're checking that out next. It's only been a week. He's old enough to look after himself. He'll surely turn up soon. They don't know that you've listened to his mother on the other end of the phone, picking up the extension more carefully than you've ever done before and hardly daring to breathe, your palm damp over the mouthpiece. You've heard her gulps and sobs as your mother tries to comfort her. You know he didn't leave a note, but you know he didn't take anything, either: not the jar of fifty pence pieces on his shelf, not his beloved guitar, not his Discman, not even – so far as they can tell – a change of clothes or underwear. You want to speak up, and ask her if maybe he's in Tokyo, but of course you can't do that, and anyway, you don't really believe in it even yourself. One night you have a nightmare that he's trapped in

Zork, and after that you find you can no longer play it because the voice that instructs and responds, making wisecracks and not-understanding, suddenly sounds too much like his. The thought that he's in there, trying to talk to you, makes your skin creep and crawl, and you take out the disk and shove it back in its sleeve and bury it right at the back of the box. You think of the pictures on his wardrobe, and you think that the whole year of *Zork* was a training in the secret messages that people are trying to tell you, that are there to be read, if only you know how; and you know, you just know, that whatever's happened to him or wherever he is, he's never coming back.

The iHole

Julian Gough

IT WAS A presentation Tuesday, and the room was full. While they waited for Thierry, they ran through a year's worth of rumours. He'd moved back in with his mother. His mother was schizophrenic. No, she'd lost her memory in a car crash. She collected, ah, butterflies? Barbies? Beanie Babies. She'd been seen wandering around a parking lot, naked... But the rumours had low energy, and soon died out. Thierry himself had no enemies, no friends, and no life that anyone knew of.

★

He'd unveiled it before most people had noticed he was in the room.

The black hole sat there, floating in mid air, beside the lectern.

Eventually somebody said '...But what does it do?'

Thierry scratched the back of his neck. 'Uh, it kind of doesn't matter what it does. Everyone will want one. Look at it.'

They looked at it. It was beautiful.

Sharif, from the hardware engineering team, reached towards it. Stopped. 'What about the interface?' he said. 'You can't really touch it, can you?'

'No. But I've already talked to, ah… design. Justin doesn't think that'll be a problem.'

'Why can I see it?' said Melissa from the strategy group.

'Positive and negative uh particles…' Of course, Melissa's background was in physics. Thierry restarted. 'Matter and antimatter particle pairs come into existence all the time, everywhere, you know – vacuum energy – but usually they annihilate each other straight away.'

'Like the Oilers and the Flames,' said Brett, ever the professional Canadian. Nobody laughed, they didn't even acknowledge it, they wanted to hear Thierry.

'Um, this is designed to suck in the antimatter, and push away the, the matter. So it radiates. But the radiation is coming from just *outside* the Schwarzschild radius, the event horizon, you see? Nothing can come back from inside the Schwarzschild radius.'

'But…' Melissa was frowning. 'Hawking discovered that small black holes evaporate, no?'

'Only incredibly small ones. And besides, if it's

losing mass you can just feed it.'

Melissa nodded. 'Have you… fed it?'

'Uh, not yet.'

Melissa leaned towards it. 'Can I?'

'Sure.'

Melissa picked up Thierry's pen from the lip of the lectern. Thierry's body almost made to reach for the pen, but only twitched slightly, as his mind cancelled the order. It was just a pen.

'So, anyway,' said Thierry. 'It's spinning, so it's stable, like a gyroscope….'

Melissa threw Thierry's pen through the air. It vanished into the black hole.

'Oh my God,' said Melissa. 'That felt...' She shook her head. 'These are going to be huge… Do it,' Melissa urged the others. 'Do it…'

It was a very clean space. No trash cans, no trash. People began to look through their pockets for old tissues, ringpulls, candy wrappers. They dropped them, threw them, flicked them into the black hole. Each time, a gasp, or startled laughter.

'Why doesn't it fall?' said Sharif. 'I mean it has a lot of mass, right?'

'That was the hardest part. It's designed to radiate boundary energy asymmetrically – downwards – enough to balance gravity. It's constantly making very fine adjustments, like a Segway.'

'Is it safe?'

'There are safety features. Filters. You don't want kids falling into them. It's too small to swallow anything larger or heavier than, you know, a melon. Anything bigger will just bounce back.'

'What about your finger?'

'If it's attached to you, it'll bounce back. It registers the whole mass.'

'So you'd have to cut up your victims,' said Brett.

Thierry smiled uneasily.

They drifted away, excited, a little giddy. Thierry was right; they all wanted one.

★

Chris got his own private presentation the next day. The recent breakup of Apple by the Department of Justice had created a huge, open space at the heart of the crowded consumer hardware business. Chris had been looking for something big, bold, and original, to take that space. This was it. He made it a priority project.

They assembled a team around Thierry. A lot of technicians under him, and some senior managers unobtrusively over him. Let's say, alongside him.

Over the next few weeks, they perfected it. Justin came in with his team, and they radically improved the interface. Made it more sensitive to human-scale movement. Now you could move it around with hand gestures. It could follow you like a balloon.

★

The prototypes were kept under the usual high security in the new building. But the original, by unspoken agreement, Thierry was allowed to keep. It floated over the white leather top of his new desk. He didn't put anything into it himself. But people would wander by, from every corner of the campus. They'd chat for a minute, then say they didn't want to disturb him, but could they… He'd nod, and they'd throw something into it. A soda can, a cigarette butt. Sometimes something wrapped up, or hidden with a hand. And then the big sigh of relief, or the sudden laugh, at the oddness, the finality, of putting anything into the black hole. The *satisfaction*.

'Well, it's not like any normal means of disposal,' Thierry would say politely.

'Yes!' They'd be giddy. 'It feels like I blasted it beyond the solar system…' '…beyond the edge of the galaxy,' '…beyond the rim of the known universe.'

'Yes,' he'd say. 'You did. It is removed from the universe.'

★

Technically, things went pretty smoothly. The biggest arguments were about what to call it. What seemed the only obvious name to Thierry was fiercely contested by some of the marketing department. In the end, Chris over-ruled marketing. 'People will hate the name. Sure. So what? It's simple and it works. People hated the name iPad, for about a week. They made every possible joke about sanitary towels – for a week. And then they got used to it.'

★

Chris launched it in February. He did it beautifully. The crowd gasped, the crowd laughed. Young people said it was the best launch they could remember. Old timers said it was as good as one of Steve's.

★

Thierry celebrated that night. The team took him to a bar in the hills west of Sunnyvale. Around 2am, he was standing outside, looking up at the stars. The black hole floated over his head. He tried to line it up with Sirius. There. The black hole bent the starlight around itself, making a tiny ring of light.

He felt his vision flashing, and he looked down, bewildered, at the joint in his right hand. Who'd given it to him? He brought it up to his eyes. Was it laced with something? The white paper, the smoke, seemed to turn blue, then red, then blue. By the time he realised it was a cop car's lights, it was too late, they had the camera on him and were filming. He flicked the joint, reflexively, toward the black hole, and it vanished from the universe.

The cops took him in and tried to frighten him for the next two, three hours, but he was very relaxed and waited it out. He had nothing on him. They let him go at dawn. He picked up the original iHole at the front desk. The young cop on duty, who'd been playing with it, feeding it paperclips, said, 'So when can I get one of these?' and Thierry gave him the tour.

★

The previews, working off the specifications Chris had announced at the launch, were sniffy as hell. Why would anyone want this? The price is all wrong. It doesn't do anything a garbage can doesn't do better, for less.

But the reviews, once people had actually tried one, were raves.

The company shipped a million iHoles, and they were sold out pretty much everywhere in three days. And the word of mouth was incredible.

★

A month later, McGowan, in the *New York Times*, wrote a sober and considered piece that basically said, it isn't perfect, but they will iterate it. Look at all the things missing from the first iPod, iPhone, iPad. 'But already it has replaced the office shredder, wastepaper baskets, your garbage can, ashtrays... Not just replaced. It's made the act of disposal sexy. My kids fight to take out the trash, and they dispose of it eggshell by eggshell, they don't want it to be over. When people love a device so much that they want to play with it, even when they don't actually have a task that requires it... the device works. The iHole is going to be a huge, global hit.'

And it was.

★

People started to bring out attachments, add ons. You could connect your iHole to the back of your mower. Watch the grass fly up, curve around it, and... vanish. One attachment – with a little ramp, a cheeseholder – turned it into a better mousetrap.

★

When the iHole 2 came out, they'd made its sensors much, much more fine-grained. Now it could tell the difference between you and the crumbs on your hands, the sand in your cracks, dandruff in your hair. You could set the filters to clean yourself with it. You could be so clean it was as though you'd never really been clean before.

★

The only negative reactions came from the environmental movement, but even they found it hard to find an angle, a tone. They came off as attacking it just because it was new.

There was something close to a backlash, when the recycling companies started to go out of business. But the company immediately ran ads showing how much landfill would be unnecessary if everybody carried an iHole. The number of incinerators that wouldn't need to be built. Smiling children played in green fields as their father dropped the picnic rubbish into the family iHole.

Then the company tweaked the iHole 3 so that it absorbed carbon dioxide from the air around it. And they dropped the price of the entry model by a hundred bucks.

At the launch, a stunning, two-minute long, fifteen million dollar film by James Cameron painted the iHole 3 as the ultimate carbon capture device. Green resistance collapsed. The company's share price doubled.

★

Then the scare stories started running. It had taken a while – iHoles were as close to tamper-proof as consumer products could get – but now people were modifying them. A man in Brazil – upset after his girlfriend left him for a woman – managed to stick his penis in a jail-broken iHole, with highly unpleasant consequences. Which he filmed for her. The clip was the most viewed in the world that year.

★

The first big court case involved a woman in New Jersey who'd modified an array of iHoles to take massive objects. She ran the operation out of a warehouse, and got caught when the stream of dumptrucks started blocking the docks. She was charged with running an unlicensed landfill. The company was subpoenaed, as an accessory.

There were months of tortuous argument, from dozens of expert witnesses. It went all the way to the Supreme Court, with more and more parties joining the case.

Liberal groups, worried about the abortion implications, defended the right to dispose of whatever you like on private property. They also argued that garbage disposal was a form of speech, protected by the First Amendment. Conservatives defended private ownership of modified iHole arrays on Second Amendment grounds.

Thierry followed the case with decreasing interest. Halfway through the Supreme Court hearing, the judges had requested iHoles, in order to understand the case. It was quite obvious they'd fallen in love with theirs instantly, and were clearly not going to rule against the company.

After a lot of closing evidence from physicists, the case was dismissed on the grounds that, even if there had been a crime, it had not been committed in this universe.

★

The first knockoffs were announced at the Consumer Electronics Show, in Las Vegas, a few weeks later. But there were stability issues, and none of the products which were announced that January made it to market that summer.

Microsoft had learned a lesson from the failure of their answer to the iPod. The Zune had sold poorly through online shops, partly because it was always last in any alphabetical list of similar products. Senior executives at Microsoft were anxious not to make that mistake again. They over-ruled their marketing department, and in late September launched the A-Hole.

But it was already too late. The iHole completely owned the market. Even expensive, well thought-out competitors were perceived as cheap, inferior copies. In the run-up to Christmas, desperate for market share, Microsoft began to sell their A-Hole at a loss. They still couldn't get penetration.

★

The unauthorised modifications began to get out of hand. In a global marketplace, this threw up some cultural differences. That autumn, in Canada, people used it to get rid of leaves.

In the USA and Mexico, the number of people found murdered dropped sharply. The number reported missing rose.

In China, protests in rural areas ceased to be a problem.

In Saudi Arabia, radical jihadists dropped Shias, German tourists, and the wrong kinds of Sunni down the hole – slowly, headfirst – and posted the videos online.

In the West Bank, settlers threw Palestinians down the hole (except on Saturdays). And vice versa (except on Fridays).

In Gaza, Hamas and Fatah spent most of their budgets on iHoles, and threw each other down the hole in such quantities that Gaza became quite peaceful, until an Israeli soldier threw a Palestinian teenager down the hole at a border crossing, and it all kicked off again.

A number of lawsuits emerged from all this. But the company made no admission of liability, and was cleared in every case. The US Supreme Court's precedent proved extremely useful. In country after country, the entire product was deemed to exist, by definition, beyond the event horizon, and therefore beyond the jurisdiction of the court, whose jurisdiction was limited to this universe.

★

At the end of the year, the amount of money Thierry received in his bonus was ridiculous. He celebrated by going to the bank, withdrawing a million dollars in cash, and throwing it, a hundred dollars at a time, into the original iHole. Then he smashed up all his furniture and fed in the pieces.

On his way to the bar that night, the cops stopped him. He thought it was to do with his mother, but it was for pot again. He was so relieved, he let them find some.

Afterwards, when the court summons arrived, he regretted it. Too late.

To avoid thinking about the court case, he lost himself in research, helping Justin work on the big problem. Eventually they solved it, by shifting the Hawking radiation into the visible spectrum. Cautiously, tweak by tweak, they turned a black hole white.

The next iteration had hardly any functional improvements, but it came out in white, and the world upgraded. Within a month, kids with the original black iHole were being jeered at in the street. Their hats, their lunch, their homework were shoved down the hole.

★

Back in court, Thierry felt proceedings weren't really real. He'd opted for jury trial. The judge and the lawyers on both sides seemed to be playing language games. Thierry couldn't see how their arguments related to empirical, objective reality. They just seemed to be sentences about paragraphs of old laws that had been written with no understanding of the strangeness and beauty of the universe.

He modified his iHole as the jury deliberated. When they came back into court and announced that they had reached their verdict, he gently lobbed his modified iHole into the jury box, and they all disappeared.

This led to a second, more serious courtcase. But precedent in iHole law was by now clear: 'If an event occurs within the boundary, information from that event cannot reach an outside observer, making it impossible to determine if such an event occurred.'

The judge in Thierry's second case determined that the first jury had reached a verdict but that it was not known yet, therefore could not be acted upon. As a verdict had been reached in the original trial, there could be no second trial. However, Thierry was ordered to restore the settings on his iHole to their original state. He did so.

Thierry was released.

★

Back at home, he didn't seem to know what to do. The house was just a shell with a futon lying on the floor of one room. Using his Swiss army knife, Thierry ripped up the futon and fed it into the black hole. It took all night.

★

At dawn, he brought the iHole to the lab and let himself in. The cleaners stared at him. He said hello, quietly. He sat at his desk, in his imposing chair, and looked at the iHole for a while. He'd stuck with the original black so long, it was coming back into fashion as a retro look.

He slowly logged into the iHole's core code, through layer after layer of security.

He modified the source code for all iHoles worldwide, and sent it out as an emergency security patch.

Something fell back out of the iHole, and bounced across the desk.

He picked it up, and looked at it. His pen. He brought the tip down to the desk's surface, and scribbled. After a hesitant, scratchy second or so, the ink came through. He stared at the tight black scribble on the white leather.

A Snickers wrapper fell on the leather beside him. Then another. As the candy wrappers and used tissues and Coke cans fell all around him, bouncing off his back, his arms, his bowed head, he wrote 'I'm sorry I'm sorry I'm sorry I'm sorry I'm sorry,' on the white leather desk, till the pen ran out of ink and the dry tip tore holes in the white skin.

Eventually the first Beanie Baby fell onto the desk. He threw the empty pen into the corner of the room, curled up in the big chair, and waited for his mother to return.

Even Pretty Eyes
Commit Crimes

M.J. Hyland

MY FATHER WAS sitting on my doorstep. He was wearing khaki shorts, his bare head was exposed to the full bore of the sun, and he was holding a pineapple. I hadn't a clue what he was doing there. He hadn't given me any warning.

As I crossed the street, I raised my hand, but his eyes were closed, and he didn't see me until I was standing right in front of him.

'Dad. What are you doing here so early?'

'Relax,' he said. 'There's nothing to worry about.'

I looked at my watch. It wasn't yet eight-thirty and I wasn't in the mood for him. I'd walked home to save on bus fares after working a ten-hour night shift and I needed a shower and sleep.

'Did you knock?'

'No,' he said. 'I didn't knock. I didn't want to wake anybody. I was just going to leave the pineapple on your doorstep, but then I sat down to rest for a minute and you turned up.'

The neighbour's dogs were barking. My father frowned at the pampas grass that grew wild along the length of the broken fence.

'Your neighbours need to train those bloody kelpies to stop barking.'

I held out my hand.

'Here, Dad. Grab hold.'

'I'm alright,' he said. 'No need.'

I'd had twenty-nine years to get used to Australia; its boiling summers, long days with no distinct parts - hot in the morning, noon and night - but I still couldn't stomach the heat or the glare that came off every footpath and every parked car. My father was the opposite. He was made better by the sun; it made him buoyant and though he was sixty-five, on that morning, I was much more beaten and tired than he'd ever been.

'Do you want to come into the flat for a minute,' I said.

'If that's alright.'

'We'd best be quiet, though. Janice won't be out of bed yet.'

But Janice wasn't home. As soon as we were inside the hall I saw she'd left the bedroom door open and it was clear the bed hadn't been slept in. I'd made the bed and it was just as I'd left it. We'd had an argument about money before I left for work

and when I was walking out the door she said,
'You're boring now, Paul.'

She said this in the cool and expert way my
mother used to say things about couples who sit in
cafés reading the newspaper and not talking to
each other. 'They're boring each other,' she used to
say. 'They're probably only days away from divorce.'

My father looked into the bedroom, just as I had
done. He suspected Janice of straying, just as he'd
suspected my mother.

'Janice must be out,' I said.

I straightened my shoulders and tried to hide
my worry and fatigue. I was at the end of a long
run of night shifts, and I wasn't in the mood for the
grilling he'd give me if he knew about my
marriage troubles.

'Where's your uniform?' he asked.

'In my locker. I don't like walking home
wearing it. I get changed first.'

'So, you have a clean one for tomorrow's
shift?'

'Yes, Dad. I have a few.'

He looked into the bedroom again. 'Where
do you think she is?'

'Keep your hat on, Dad. She's probably just
popped out to do some shopping.'

I owed my father some money, and mentioning
shops was a mistake. He was well-off and enjoyed
his riches, but he didn't like giving money away,
not without arrangements for its 'fair return'.

When I was eighteen my father asked me to have a drink with him. It was the first time he'd asked to meet me in a pub and he picked the day and time of the meeting months in advance.

'It's time we had a proper man-to-man chat,' he said.

It was a perfect spring day, a gentle day, and we sat in the corner of the dark pub under a TV screen, in a suburb miles from his surgery, and even further away from my university digs.

'It's time I told you a few home-truths,' he said.

'OK,' I said. 'Go ahead.'

'Well, for starters, I knew your mother was up to no good years before she left us.'

As far as I was concerned, she hadn't left *us* when I was ten years old, she'd left *him*. She'd got sick of him and found somebody else. I was only ten, but I wasn't stupid. I'd heard her say, 'Men shouldn't talk as much as you do, Richard.'

My father sipped his beer slowly and looked at the TV screen above my head.

'She was a very good liar, your mother,' he said.

I was too angry to speak. What he'd said got me in the gut, a weird kind of wetness low in my stomach. I'd have got blind drunk that day if I'd had some spare money of my own but I had to listen to him curse my mother with nothing but a warm glass of beer froth in front of me.

When he came back to the table after ordering another round, he put the drinks down on our corner table and sat close and, after a moment, as though he was a different person, he put his hand on my knee.

'I'll tell you something now,' he said. 'Even pretty eyes commit crimes. You should bear that in mind when you start making lady friends.'

'Right,' I said.

'You prefer ladies, don't you?'

'Of course I do,' I said. 'Jesus Christ!'

My father didn't like sitting close to people, and he didn't like touching, and said he loathed displays of affection of any kind, but he was sitting very close, and his hand stayed on my knee a bit too long, and he softly squeezed, and my knee got hotter and hotter, and he kept looking at me, as though waiting for me to do something, and I had an idea that he was going to ask if we could have sex, father and son. It was a crazy idea, but I was certain of it. I moved my leg.

'Well then,' he said, 'you've been warned. You thought your mother was an angel because she looked like one, but you were completely wrong about that.'

I didn't want to hear any more. I told him I needed to use the toilet and I went to the bar and used the last of my money to pay for our drinks. I wasn't going to say goodbye, I couldn't stand him anymore, but he came round the corner, and saw me.

'What are you doing?' he said.

'I need to go back to Uni. I just remembered I have to meet my tutor.'

My father and I had lived alone together for seven years and, for seven years, when he got home from work, I'd be stuck with him, trapped with his talking in the kitchen or lounge, and if he wanted me when I went into my bedroom, he'd barge in, and I'd have to yawn my head right off its hinges to get rid of him. Nearly every weekend I'd pretend to be going into the city to see a film with friends and instead, catch the bus to an internet café three suburbs away, and drink coffee and play games online.

He followed me to the front door of the pub. 'Did you hear what I said? Were you listening?'

'Yes, but I have to go to a lecture.'

'You're a stinking liar,' he said. 'I'm staying on and I'll finish these beers. I don't like people who waste time and money. Do you follow me?'

'Yes,' I said.

He opened the door for me, and saw me out to the street.

We saw very little of each other after that spring afternoon; once or twice a year, my birthday and Christmas, but that changed when I married Janice. On our wedding day, at a small outdoor ceremony by the lake, he gave me our wedding gift; a Tartan picnic flask, six blue plastic cups, and a matching rug.

'You'll have a family of your own, soon,' he said. 'And I want to help you along. I can help you get on with things. I can help you sort things out.'

After the wedding, he formed a habit of stopping by the flat, donating furniture, giving me loans, calling me late in the night and saying things like, 'I'm just around the corner. Have you got a minute?'

And here he was again, only two months since his last visit, standing beside my kitchen table and holding a pineapple in the crook of his arm.

I turned my back to him and checked the whiteboard on the fridge to see if Janice had left me a message. She hadn't. I pretended to check the clock over the sink and looked into the backyard. Her bike was leaning against the shed, but her helmet wasn't in the basket. She might be gone for good and my father would be here to see it happen.

As I turned round to face him, he gave me the pineapple, offered it to me as though it were something of great value.

'It fell off the tree when I was heading home last night,' he said. 'What a glorious country, eh?'

'I don't really like pineapples, Dad. Why don't you give it to somebody at work?'

'Give it back to me, then. It's not going to waste.'

I gave it back to him.

'You should eat more fruit,' he said.

'You're right,' I said. 'I should.'

I thought he was going to leave but he sat at the table and put the pineapple in his lap. He was going to stay, and there was nothing I could do about it.

'What do you want to drink?' I said. 'Will a cup of tea do?'

'That'd be nice.'

I opened the fridge and looked out to the backyard again. The neighbour's ginger cat was curled up, asleep, on the Greek family's trampoline.

'Sorry, Dad. There's no milk.'

There was always milk in the fridge. Janice bought two litres every night when she went to the 7-Eleven on the corner for her cigarettes.

'Then I'll have water,' he said. 'Do you have ice?'

'You don't want a beer?'

'Christ, no,' he said. 'It's too early. I'm working today.'

'What time do you start?'

'I'm supposed to be there by nine. But there's no mad rush. I've arranged for the locum to do the mornings.'

There was no ice in the ice-tray, but I rummaged in the freezer as though there was hope it might be found. The breeze from the frost took some of the heat off my hands.

'There's no ice,' I said.

'Forget the water, then. I'll suck on one of these.'

He took a packet of *Fisherman's Friends* from

the back pocket of his khaki shorts.

'Do you want one?'

'No thanks, Dad. They make me cough.'

As soon as I sat at the table, he stood and went to the sink and put the pineapple on the draining board, tried to stand it upright. When it toppled, he held its bottom and moved it round 'til he was sure it wouldn't budge.

'Thanks for the pineapple,' I said. 'Janice will love it.'

'Does she usually go out so early in the morning?'

'Sometimes,' I lied. 'She likes going for walks.'

'Is she still selling buttons?'

'No, she quit. And it wasn't buttons, it was sewing equipment...'

'I know that.'

He sat down again, but didn't pull his chair under the table. I thought he'd be leaving soon.

'How have you been?' he said. 'How are you keeping?'

'I've been well-enough, thanks, Dad. The nights are hard, but I like the quiet hours when the patients are sleeping. And the walk home is good.'

He looked at the ceiling fan.

'Is that broken?'

'Yes. The landlord's coming to fix it soon.'

He looked at the window.

'Didn't she leave you a note or anything? Didn't she tell you where she was going?'

'No, Dad. I'm not her minder.'

I sat up in the chair and put my shoulders back, tried to make my body look bigger, tried to hide my panic. But it made no difference. I was work-wrecked and nervous and he could see it. Janice was gone somewhere, and it might be for good this time.

'How about you, Dad?'

'I could use a bit more help. The locum's pretty good, but my secretary's always behind. Things are getting to be too much for us. I've been wondering if I should retire.'

We were silent then and the only sound came from the traffic in Ormond Road, the delivery trucks beeping as they reversed out of the Mornflake warehouse. He wasn't troubled by the silence, or the lack of something to do with his hands. He was tidy and ambitious and he liked his own company. Even a stranger could see it; the way he sat with his hands on the knees of his khaki shorts, the creases just as they were when he pulled them, brand new from the box.

'Maybe you need a new secretary,' I said.

'Don't be daft, son. I've spent too long training her. Anyway, the patients like her. She keeps teddy bears behind the desk for the kiddies.'

'That's good then, Dad,' I said. 'Surely the fact that the patients like your secretary's much more important than paperwork.'

'You're right, son,' he said. 'Of course, you're right.'

The baby in the flat upstairs started howling.

'It's too hot in here,' I said.

I stood and opened the back door and, as soon as it was open, the ginger cat jumped off the trampoline and ran into the kitchen and sniffed at the cupboard door under the sink, walked to the door and looked at us for a moment, then sat.

'Is that yours?' he said.

'No. It belongs to the upstairs neighbour.'

'Why does it come in here?'

'That's what cats do,' I said. 'It wants food, I suppose.'

'It stinks,' he said. 'Is it neutered? You should tell those Greeks upstairs that neutering is a relatively cheap and simple operation.'

There was no air coming through the kitchen door and the backs of my knees were sweating.

I stood up from the table.

'Listen, Dad. I might have a bit of a sleep now, if that's alright.'

'Won't you be waking up again soon?' he said. 'When Janice gets home?'

'Not necessarily. I'm a heavy sleeper.'

He stood and looked over at the pineapple on the draining board.

'I'll get out of your hair then, will I?'

We faced each other across the table, and we were breathing in unison.

'OK. Stay for a bit,' I said. 'I can sleep later. Let's go into the lounge room.'

I stopped in the hallway and told him I'd be in soon.

'I just want to open the bedroom window.'

Janice had cleared out most of her clothes. I couldn't check the bedside drawers, without my father wondering what I was doing, but I knew the drawers would be empty, too. She'd threatened leaving, but I didn't believe she would, not like this, not this suddenly, not without a final warning, not without a last chance. People didn't end marriages this way, without warning, without second chances.

I got two glasses of orange juice and brought them into the lounge. My father was standing by the window and he'd unclenched his jaw, let his mouth hang open. I saw how he might look in repose, when there was nobody else around. He'd let me see him, not as strong, and not as calm. He was thinking about my mother, and I sensed it there in his slackened mouth and, for a moment, I thought of her too, the memory that always came to me first, though I didn't want it to.

It was a few months before she left home, a winter's day, and the three of us were eating lunch in a café. She told the waitress she wanted something that wasn't on the menu. She asked for a 'large onion sandwich'. The waitress was still at our table when my father laughed at her. 'Precisely how large is a large onion?' he said.

My mother got out of her seat.

'The waitress knew what I meant,' she said. 'Everybody else knew what I meant.'

He tried to apologise, as he often did, by saying, 'Oh, pet. Don't feel that way.'

She came round to my father's side of the table. She'd hung her coat over the back of his chair and she needed him to sit forward to get at it.

'Move,' she said.

He turned round to her, put his hand on her arm, and tried to console her as best he could, as he often did, by holding onto a part of her.

'I said move,' she said, 'you slow, deaf pig! I need my coat.'

My father didn't move quickly enough. She wrenched the coat from behind his back.

'You're embarrassing me, Richard,' she said. 'Get off my bloody coat!'

I stood in the lounge room doorway and held the glasses of orange juice and looked at him, waited for him to see me.

'Oh, hi,' he said. 'I've turned on the fan for you.'

'Thanks, Dad. Here's your OJ.'

I sat down on the end of the settee and he sat in the armchair near the door. As we sat, we crossed our legs, left over right, a genetic tic, something we always did when we sat down.

'So, where do you think that young wife of

yours has got to?'

'She's probably meeting a friend for coffee or something.'

He looked at his watch. 'It's very early for that.'

I said nothing, and he sat forward, moved his legs round so that his knees and feet were aimed in my direction.

'I think I'll call Janice,' I said. 'I'll ask her to bring some milk and ice back with her.'

'Alright,' he said. 'I should be heading off soon anyway.'

'OK,' I said and felt the phone warm in my hand.

He waited for me to check for messages, but there were none. She was gone.

'She's on her way home,' I said. 'She says she'll be back soon.'

'Where is she?'

'I don't know yet. But I think I'll try and get some sleep now.'

I thought he'd leave then, but he didn't. He was going to stick it out, wait with me until she came home - or didn't.

'I've been meaning to ask you,' he said. 'Have you given any more thought to taking the exam?'

He was talking about the mature-age medical school exam. He'd reminded me of it the last time we met, and the time before that.

'Not yet,' I said, 'but I will.'

'Do you think you'll work as a nurse for the rest of your life?'

'I might, Dad. I like it.'

'How's your blood-pressure been of late?'

'Normal, Dad. It's normal.'

'Do you still get those dizzy spells? Maybe while I'm here I could check your pulse?'

'I can check my own bloody pulse. There's no need.'

'You look a bit flushed. A bit iffy around the gills.'

'There's nothing wrong with me. I'm just real hot, Dad. It's just stuffy in here. I feel like I'm wearing a bear suit.'

'I see,' he said. 'You never did warm to the heat.'

He laughed at himself, like a school-boy.

'Good one,' I said. 'That's a good one.'

We were silent and he scratched his arm while looking out the window. A Mornflake truck was reversing out of the factory warehouse.

'There might be fleas in here,' he said, 'from that cat. Have you been bitten?'

'No. I haven't been bitten. It was probably a mozzie.'

'There's a lot of sand,' he said. 'In the carpet.'

We lived fifteen minutes from Bondi Beach and that's part of the reason why we paid so much rent for such a cramped, gloomy flat. I wanted to move out to the suburbs, just for a few years, and save some money for an air-conditioner and a trip back to London, but Janice couldn't stand the stench of the suburban sticks and so we stayed and bought three fans; so that made four fans, including the overhead in the kitchen that was busted.

I looked at him and jiggled my glass, swirled the juice round as though it had ice in it, and said nothing about the sand.

'You can check your mobile phone again if you want,' he said.

'I'm not worried, Dad. She'll be here in a minute.'

He stood. 'I should be going,' he said. 'I'll see myself out.'

'OK, Dad. Thanks for coming over. I'm sorry I wasn't very good company.'

'You're tired, that's all. You've never liked the heat.'

We stood in the hallway, near the front door. His hands were stuffed inside his khaki pockets and he didn't look like he was ready to go. In this in-between state, this waiting, this not coming or going, he'd usually be the one to make the first move to action. But on that morning, he stood stock still, and looked at me. I didn't want to speak, and he didn't either, so I opened the front door and stepped outside and waited for him to follow. I was in a bad state, sweating and nervous, and even though I didn't want to be left alone, I didn't know how to be this way with him watching me.

'Goodbye,' I said.

'Goodbye, son.'

I'd already turned to go back inside when he stepped back onto the porch and took hold of me. He hugged me, long enough for me to feel what went on beneath his chest, and I closed my eyes as he held me, and there was no rush from either of us to get it over with, and I held him with the same strength as he held me.

He let go first, but it wasn't to be rid of me. He wanted to say something. He took hold of my wrist.

'I hope you can find a way out of this situation, son. I wish you luck.'

And so he knew Janice had gone, and he'd probably known for a long time that she'd leave me, and maybe he hadn't come to rub my nose in it. Maybe it wasn't that at all.

'OK,' I said. 'OK, Dad.'

Saying 'OK' said nothing, and meant nothing, but as I held my breath, and watched him walk down the path, I hoped he'd realise that I wanted to say more, and that I just didn't know how to take the chance. He'd know, wouldn't he, that I was too surprised to speak? Maybe he'd have seen that I was too afraid to do anything, or say anything, that might bring my emotions to the boil. I was too busy shuddering to say anything more, and I hoped he knew that, and that he realised, that morning, I loved him.

The Goose Father

Krys Lee

EVEN AFTER SOONAH and their two children had left Seoul for Boston, Gilho Pak denied that he was what the newspapers dubbed a 'goose father', one of those men who faithfully sent money to his family living overseas. The original goose fathers, the term signifying their journey from one country to another, were Korean men who had been drafted or volunteered as mercenary soldiers for the U. S. army in Vietnam, and sent their salaries back to their family. But back then, there had been few jobs and a national landscape of poverty. Gilho was not a goose; he was entirely stationary. He was a successful accountant who did not associate himself with the Vietnam mercenaries, much less the so-called goose fathers reduced to eating ramen for dinner; those men so dishonest they had other women in their wives' absence, men who collapsed from strokes, unearthed in their homes weeks later by neighbours, men less than men in their solitude. Unlike those fathers, his family's absence made Gilho even more upright and correct in his behaviour. Sex? He had never understood the fuss. And what about Junho, his ten-year-old son, and his daughter, Jinhee, in American private schools, his wife's language-school tuition that qualified her for a student visa, their living expenses? He'd had the foresight of a self-made man, and made sound investments before the country's financial crisis in 1998.

Still, despite the books he finally had time to read and the spotless flooring he could maintain, loneliness made him feel like a house teetering on an eroding cliff. He dreaded the evening quiet of his apartment, and resorted to making phone calls to friends as he moved from room to room that rebuked him with their emptiness. The night he woke up hugging his daughter's filthy baseball mitt, he decided to put a stop to this nonsense. So, six months after separation from his family, he advertised, interviewed several candidates, then settled for a tenant, a boy who seemed as alone as Gilho.

The next week when Gilho came home, the tenant was sitting on the doormat. He had two suitcases stacked in front of him and a goose the size of an overfed house cat in his arms. A goose of all creatures, as if the boy was mocking Gilho. The bird shifted and revealed a splash of white paint across its dung-coloured chest, as if God – though Gilho no longer believed in God – had slipped up with his paintbrush.

Gilho charged past the lanky boy and opened the door, but Wuseong scrambled to his feet and grasped his shoulder with his free hand. Gilho was about to dismiss him, call off their agreement, but he froze as he took in the boy's anxious rosebud lips, the drooping pine needle scar that marred his chin, his shaved monkish head. Somehow, despite the goose's grime, the boy managed to look so clean. He was almost too pretty to be a boy, Gilho thought before he escaped into the apartment.

At the threshold the boy hovered and looked helplessly into the museum-white living room, just as Gilho had twenty years earlier when he, a farmer's son from the island of Geoje, had been looking for cheap accommodations. He had been the first one in the family to attend college, and the first person in his village to be accepted by Seoul National University, the nation's most prestigious institution. His father had killed two pigs in Gilho's honour and held a party for the village, complete with a giant banner announcing his son's achievements. Gilho had been an earnest student afraid of failing his family, overwhelmed by gratitude when a wealthy, popular girl on campus, now his wife, began paying attention to him. But over the years, he had excised the farm boy, stamped out his provincial traces, and become used to this new him.

'This goose – you didn't mention a goose,' Gilho said. 'Do you know how many germs it carries? It'll infest my home.'

'Pak ajeoshi.' The boy's address for older men was as supple as fresh rice cakes. He clutched the goose to his gaunt chest, and his eyes opened wide in alarm. 'Oh, you can't turn away a goose with only one good wing – she just found me! That's like Superman without his cape. Like General Yi Sun-shin without his Turtle Ship. I swear she'll be out of the way on the balcony.'

Gilho had accepted a month's rent in advance. There was his balcony of horticultural treasures, but he was not a person to violate his commitments. He sank into the leather sofa.

'I advertise for a tenant; I get a dirty little bird.'

Wuseong stroked the goose with long pianist's fingers. Like a tamed animal, the goose rested its head against the boy's thin chest. Then the boy scuttled over to the balcony, slid open the glass door, and deposited the goose in the middle of Gilho's plants. It stretched its short tuber neck and disappeared behind a waxy green frond. After waving to it, the boy hefted his suitcases up and deposited them in the spare room. He returned hunched, one tentative foot at a time, so different from the way Gilho had become: a man used to having his way, a man used to making demands.

'Please, ajeoshi,' Wuseong said. He blushed like a newlywed. 'It's eight o'clock at night and we don't have anywhere to go.'

They were an incongruous pair: a man whose gaze did not seem to take in anything more than it needed to; whose very walk was efficient and with purpose; the kind of man who seemed to have ambled out of his mother's womb fully formed. Wuseong teetered like a beanstalk when he walked; his speech hovered precariously between leisure and panic. He watched in awe as Gilho completed fifty push-ups while reading a newspaper spread flat on the ground.

Gilho stood up, his breathing even, as if his body had been at rest.

Gilho said, 'If that bird eats my plants, it's leaving first thing tomorrow morning.'

'Goodnight, my ajeoshi.'

Gilho shook his head, and turned away.

Precisely at six the next morning, Gilho headed to the balcony with a steaming mug of green tea. He cultivated, among other plants, cacti, specialising in Mexican Tehuacan desert specimens that he kept warm through the forbidding winters with a special heating unit. For a decade he had found refuge each morning in this forest of cacti, where, before facing the greyness of his responsibilities, he read out loud half a dozen sijo, three-line classical poems that made him shiver with their beauty. But when he slid open the glass door, the goose fixed its gelatinous eyes on him and honked. It was resting on a shelf next to a potted *Aloe bellatula*. Alarmed, he pumped his arms at the goose. One wing dragged crookedly as if broken, and the other, billowing like a dirty white parachute, struck him in the face.

Gilho fled from the bean goose, the mutt of all birds. He was a forty-six-year-old accountant, an age and a profession that in their society commanded respect. He had relinquished so many possible selves to rescue his children from Korea's university exam hell and his wife from the crippling anxiety of the education disease, and the boy dared taunt this so-called goose father with a goose; he deserved better than this mockery!

He hunted down Wuseong.

Wuseong was in the kitchen flipping a scallion pancake in the air. His motions were languid and confident; like all of them, a different person when he was alone. Seeing Wuseong with the washcloth perched on his head like a chef's hat, his singular pleasure in the browning edges of the pancake, made Gilho forget his anger.

'Surprise!' Wuseong said. 'You haven't had a homemade meal for some time, I'm sure.'

Since Soonah had left, Gilho had resorted to buying egg and toast or a roll of kimbap at vendors' stands; seeing the steaming food made him feel sentimental. It was also uncomfortable, seeing a man performing a woman's role.

'But– I don't have anything for you,' he said.

'You can write me a poem!' Wuseong looked hopeful.

Gilho felt a phantom pain at the word. Poem. It had been years since anyone had talked about poems with him. He had belonged to the literature club on campus; some of those friends had become Korea's most exciting writers, but while they had risked and struggled, he had built himself a fortress of security and accepted the changes it had exacted from him.

'How did you know I write – wrote poetry? No one knows that about me.'

The boy flipped the pancake once, twice, before saying, 'I read your first book of poems.'

'My only book of poems.'

'Your only book of poems.' He clasped his hands in a kind of prayer. 'I looked and looked... why wasn't there a second?'

'I didn't have a second in me... there was only a first,' he admitted. 'So that's why you went and found me? To see what this old dinosaur who once wrote a few poems is doing these days?'

'Yes.'

'Well, now you know. He's an accountant with a faraway family who reads more than he should.'

'Ajeoshi, don't be angry.' His hands fluttered, graceful and nervous. 'Those poems carved me out.'

Gilho wasn't angry, just ashamed.

Wuseong inhaled the strong perfume of fish and bean paste stew. 'You should eat.'

Gilho obliged and tried the typical family breakfast: the stir-fried garlic stems and seasoned vegetables and roots were rich with flavour; the haddock was grilled to gold; the steaming communal pot of dwenjang stew had a complex base of anchovies, garlic, seaweed, and mushrooms that changed on the tongue with time. The food, doing what only good food was capable of, helped him relax.

Gilho set his chopsticks down. 'You could open a restaurant.'

Wuseong giggled and touched two fingers to his lips.

'That will never happen. I despise people, but I like cooking for you.'

Gilho turned away shyly. 'I've never heard anything so strange.'

'Well, I don't really hate-hate people. I'm too melodramatic,' Wuseong said, and smiled. 'It's a character flaw. I have a lot of those.'

He sat back delicately, as if afraid that his weight would break the chair. But only long enough to suck a grain of rice off his chopsticks before he leaped up again. He set aside a bowl of lettuce and seeds, stuck a plastic daisy into a leaf, then admired the effect. Gilho stared as the boy tiptoed to the balcony to feed the goose fresh lettuce and potato wedges; its orange-banded bill the size of a kid's trowel swooped down as if to kiss the boy's palm.

Watching the boy, Gilho felt a little dizzy. Wuseong belonged to no category of people that he recognised, and it disturbed Gilho's hard-won world order.

When Wuseong returned with the goose in one arm, Gilho pushed his chair back and snatched his briefcase, still chewing the last spoonful of rice.

He said, 'Gomab-ne. Breakfast was filling, but don't do this again.'

The boy struggled to maintain his smile; Gilho halted. He had not meant to be unkind. At the interview, he had learned that the boy's mother had passed away with kidney failure; his father he had lost contact with years ago. There was only the goose.

He said, 'I mean, I don't want to waste your time.'

Wuseong brightened with shy pleasure; like a boy unused to kindness, he was so easy to please. He shouted thank you and leaned forward so dangerously that Gilho leaped back to escape the hug. The boy frantically waved his free hand in the air as if Gilho were embarking on a long journey.

Over the next month Gilho learned that Wuseong was not only a skilled cook and a tamer of wildlife, but also an accomplished photographer, a collector of useless, arcane facts, a three-time employee of the month at Lotteria Burgers, and an amateur director who had shot two above-average short films on a borrowed camcorder, each made for less than the price of a cup of coffee. But Wuseong's immoderate passions made him quick to panic. At night Gilho heard him making disturbed talk in his sleep, sometimes crying out, his voice lashing through the silence. He spent weeks painting miniature boxes, then threw them away. All his closest friends, he said, were in jail; Gilho did not ask him any more about this. Perhaps because of the chaos of his past life, Wuseong seemed to delight in Gilho's solidity. All that was ordinary about Gilho – chewing an apple twenty-five times with each bite, reading while blow-drying his hair – was for the boy admirable, mysterious. As for Gilho, he often found himself at work wondering at this boy who didn't disguise his uncertainty, his eagerness to please, his poverty, everything that Gilho had worked so hard to hide. It was as if the only thing he knew how to be was genuine.

One morning he walked in on Wuseong talking to the goose.

'He's shy, my ajeoshi,' said the boy.

My ajeoshi. This time, the use of the possessive made Gilho flush. He said, 'And now you know how to interpret goose talk?'

The boy became radiant. 'She's not a goose, she's my mother.'

'Your mother?'

He shook his head to laugh, but he stopped when the boy disappeared behind a jumping cholla cactus.

'And what exactly is your mother saying to you?'

'I'm still learning how to understand it myself.'

'I start humouring you, bringing back home bags of chopped salad and sunflower seeds for the goose, and you start seeing your mother?'

The boy popped out from behind a swollen

cluster of cactus spines. 'She promised me she'd come back, and she did. That's what matters.'

Gilho shook his head. He said, 'No, it's not possible.'

The boy's nervous hands ruffled the goose's muscle of a neck; it angled toward the boy, submitted to its caretaker.

Gilho embarked on an awkward conversation concerning the cycle of life and death. He tried to be as gentle as he knew how. God? Allah? Buddha? Mudang? Wuseong retreated to the corner of ferns. He told the boy that all religions were ancient tricks aimed at parting you from your money, as if the boy were twelve and not twenty-two. 'I wish you were right, but this isn't the answer,' Gilho concluded. 'A goose is finally a goose, no matter what you want it to be.'

The boy's large eyes emerged over the ferns, his expression quizzical and unconvinced. He merely said, 'I'm going to make you believe.'

'I believe in helping people,' Gilho said. 'In responsibility. In family. And our country. But this is only a goose!'

'You don't need to justify yourself.' The boy smiled the kind of smile that made Gilho's face heat up. 'You're saying this because you care about me. It makes me happy.'

All he knew was that Wuseong did not leave him alone. After work or rehearsals on a comic adaptation of *Hamlet* (Gilho had not known that it was possible), the boy came directly home and flustered Gilho by skating around the kitchen with soapy sponges tied to his feet while chanting ancient Buddhist sutras on reincarnation, which forced Gilho to childishly cover his ears with his hands, though more often Gilho would spend an evening listening to Wuseong read out loud his favourite poems; the boy, to add to his prodigious talents, had a voice with the clear tenor of a church bell. Another time, Gilho came home and found Wuseong asleep, curled up on the hardwood floor without a pillow or blanket, and no yo underneath him, and when Gilho woke him up, the boy looked straight at him and said, 'Everywhere I go, a road,' before falling immediately back to sleep. The line reminded Gilho that he had, finally, lacked the courage to trust the person he had wanted to be; he walked away to recover from vertigo. When he spoke of the boy's strangeness to Soonah on the phone, she said reasonably (she was always reasonable), 'Why don't you find another tenant?'

Gilho could only wonder. In a country where a university degree made you respectable, the boy had dropped out because he wasn't being taught anything. He had thespian ambitions; he raised crippled animals for fun. His idealism couldn't last. But what might have happened if Gilho had not married and scrambled to provide Soonah with the life that she and her parents, that everyone, expected, if he had not been so susceptible to her fear of risk, of failure, of others' eyes, all fears that were his own?

Two months into the boy's stay, Gilho was persuaded to visit a local noraebaang★ with Wuseong. He had come home to the boy weeping about a documentary on the fate of krill whales, and in distress, Gilho had offered to cheer him up.

The noraebaang hall was lit with last year's Christmas lights.

'So you want a baang for the hour?' A woman leaned over the counter, outraging Gilho's aesthetics with her silicone monstrosities.

Wuseong nodded, knocking gently against Gilho as his body swayed to a silent music. He kept saying, 'We're having so much fun,' after the soju they'd shared at the drinking tent just before. Somehow this friendship with a boy half his age had become possible though people with two years' difference between them called each other 'junior' or 'senior' but rarely friends. Wuseong had no barriers; he was too guileless, Gilho thought, too trusting, and he found himself worrying about how the world would hurt him.

They were assigned a room that smelled vaguely of gym socks. As soon as the door closed Wuseong zipped open his oversize backpack and withdrew the goose. He told Gilho not to worry because in this noraebaang people did whatever they pleased, but Gilho worried because that was his nature. Still, they sang from the book of songs

★ Private room for karaoke-style entertainment; literally 'song room'.

sticky with soft drinks they drank. Wuseong plucked a pink wig off the video seat and put it on; he shook the tambourine while cavorting on the red velour couch. Gilho sang a famous folk ballad and cheered when he received a score of 100 from the machine. Even the goose, Gilho hated to admit, seemed to lumber to the music. He was feeling free and almost bohemian when he went searching for a bathroom and a girl with a large satin bow in her hair slipped past him into a room of three men. Maybe if they had enough to drink they would go somewhere else and have sex that night, the four of them.

He returned, quieter. Wuseong had lain down across the couch with his legs propped up, his face pink from the rushing blood. When he saw Gilho, he blew him a kiss.

Gilho said, 'You really don't care what people think about you, do you?'

Wuseong considered this. 'Not really, no.'

'I've always cared about the good opinion of others,' Gilho said. He had once been proud of this.

'What's wrong with that?' Wuseong sat upright. 'You have people who care about your opinions.'

He stared at the boy's calloused hands. When Wuseong straightened, Gilho looked up at his face, at the scar, which, he had begun to suspect, could also be the work of a blade. The face was young and willful, it was tired out with what it had seen. It made you want to believe. He found himself staring at the rosy flesh of the boy's lips as Wuseong leaned in, his face inching closer to Gilho's. Gilho shuddered, imagined his lips against Wuseong's lips. He slapped the boy instead.

Wuseong staggered backward, his hand cupping his cheek. Gilho's chest tightened like the beginning of a heart attack. A terrible loneliness spiked through him as he looked at the boy.

'Who are you?' said Gilho. 'What are you doing to my life?'

Wuseong bowed repeatedly in apology. An elephantine tear slid down the slant of his cheek. Gilho's heart exploded with language, but he was locked into silence, searching for words, when Wuseong scooped up the goose and leaped away and out of the noraebaang, as graceful as a bird taking flight.

At work the next morning, Wuseong's look of alarm, the shadow of Gilho's palm across his face, haunted Gilho. He composed excuses for his behaviour on company letterhead, then an hour later fed the pages into a paper shredder. He thought of his wife and children. Once he completed the half day's accounts, he hurried home. By the time he unlocked the front door he had convinced himself that nothing had happened, which was not difficult; raised in a media environment and around conversations where such feelings did not officially exist, he could not fathom them. But when he discovered that

Wuseong had disappeared, goose in tow, Gilho sat watching the empty veranda until the sun came up.

He called in sick for the first time in his working life. He trudged through December's first snow, a stickiness that turned to slush as it hit the pavement, past the homeless camped inside Seoul Station, past the wealthy clientele – Soonah's people – on gallery row near Gyeongbokgung Palace, past a platoon of soldiers, mostly college boys fulfilling compulsory military service, surrounding the U.S. embassy, past the shivering applicants queued up all day for elusive American visas, as the wind cut through his long underwear, disturbed his hair, and left him disoriented. On impulse he snuck into the nearest broker's office.

The manager with a bald spot the size of a dessert plate pulled out laminated charts. As he directed Gilho's attention to a graph with a laser pen he whipped out from his velvet jacket, Gilho thought of Soonah, their children, and the 457 days that he had so far spent without them. Business-investment visa, skilled-worker visa, education visa, visas, visas, visas.

'You're lucky!' the man said, though Gilho did not feel lucky.

'With your background you have so many options.'

After the consultation Gilho signed the contract. For a green card, for escape, he was prepared to sell the apartment and stocks to reinvest in a country already fat on the world's wealth. Only then he saw too clearly how it would be: he would be a stuttering dwarf in a land of blond giants; he would arm himself behind a liquor store counter for the rest of his days. He would lie next to his wife, a stranger forever to him. This was no true escape. As Gilho ripped up the contract, he thought of the goose in its glassed-in balcony, ferociously defending its little bit of space.

He walked through the forest of skyscrapers into the slums of Chongyecheon, where shopkeepers weaved through traffic on bicycles and peddlers sold domestic porn films that showed little more than a mosaic of faceless body parts. Later, behind the Chongryangri Lotte Department Store, two prostitutes in Technicolor halter tops dashed out of their window displays and began their sales pitch. While peering left and right for the indifferent police (there had been yet another theoretical crackdown), he picked the one with long, straight hair, long legs, a little baby fat. He kept his hands firmly cupped around her pear-shaped breasts, but each time he blinked, the curve of her waist became a boy's hips. When she asked in a stale voice, 'What is it about me, ajeoshi?' he could not tell her the truth. Her eyes reminded him of Wuseong's.

On Wednesday Wuseong still had not returned. Gilho called the police on Thursday and found himself repeating to the impatient policeman that the boy was 'memorable'. On Friday, after struggling with the tidy figures scrolling down his work monitor, he arrived late for his college alumni gathering in Yeoido. His friend Taeyeong greeted him with a slap on the shoulder and said, 'I thought the goose got you.'

Gilho almost left the barbecue restaurant there and then, but instead squeezed his friend's shoulder as he sat down.

They took turns pouring one another's shot glasses with the clear rice whiskey they had drunk together for over twenty years.

They were all born in the same year, 1960, so they could speak ban-mal to one another, they could be comfortable together.

'Geombe!' they said.

'One shot!' a friend named Duik shouted, so they clicked their glasses, downed their drinks, then held the glasses upside down over their heads to show that they were empty.

They ate small chunks of roasted pork straight off the charcoal grill with garlic and wrapped in lettuce leaves. The owner's caged-up pet pig looked on. Gilho wondered briefly if it could smell the flesh of its own kind. He had been to this restaurant several times, but he hadn't considered the pig before. This perspective, he thought, was also what Wuseong opened up in him.

Jonghun to his right poured him beer mixed with soju.

'Friend, it's too early to drink poktan-ju,'

Gilho said. 'We haven't even gotten to our second bar!'

But you should never refuse a drink from a friend, so he accepted the glass.

They were drinking; they were happily forgetting; they were slowly reaching the stage when they were no longer individuals and more like members of a group; the uri, the we in which everything dissolved: Duik's mother's death, Gilho's and Taeyeong's departed families, Sangwon's hostile marriage, Minjun's fragile solvency.

As the men drank, what seemed like a world of young people drifted past the large windows; at the next table a group of university students drank, still able to do anything and go anywhere, or become anyone.

Duik sighed. 'Remember when we couldn't pay the bill and they hauled us to the police station – what was it, five in the morning?'

'Or when we ran out of money and walked six kilometres back home?'

'That was nothing compared with military service. They would keep us awake five days in a row –'

'For me it was a week.'

'They'd give us a tiny bowl of water in the middle of summer after we'd run fifteen miles, and tell us to wash with it.'

'Everyone was so thirsty we'd fight to drink water from the toilets.'

'Now they get real food and cry when their squadron leader hits them.'

'Koreans need to be beat.'

'If they don't get beat, nothing gets done.'

'They say the young kids these days get in taxis and run away without paying. Young people these days, they have no ui-ri. They've got no honour.'

And yet they envied the young.

Within another hour, as was the custom, they moved to a bar for icha, the second round. Duik, his hair a glacial white since he'd turned thirty, stood up and sang into an empty soju bottle. Minjun picked through all the vegetables and ate only the chunks of cod in the spicy fish egg stew until another whacked him across the head.

When they talked about women, Gilho became quiet; when they'd had enough soju, they scrutinized their server's breasts.

Taeyeong said, 'It's like visiting a brothel without paying for it.'

His voice was merry, but his face wore the cost of two years' separation from his family.

Gilho looked up, his face bleak.

Taeyeong gripped his hand in mistaken sympathy. His wife and children had also left for America; he, too, understood what sacrifices it took to free your children from the sixteen hours of mindless daily cramming at school and after-school institutes that ran past midnight, the special Oriental medicines to keep them awake for college entrance exam studies, the temptation of suicide. But Gilho had been avoiding Soonah's calls for the past week.

The men kissed one another on the cheeks,

their hands across one another's shoulders and backs. Taeyeong said, 'My chingu,' and kissed Gilho on the lips. They had attended boys' schools, served in the military, and worked in corporations run like the army; they were more at ease around men. They were friends, they were men with ui-ri, loyal, steadfast men, and for their generation, that meant that they would underwrite one another's debts if asked, they would die for one another if needed.

Minjun, who had been sleeping with his head on the table for the last half hour, rubbed his eyes, yawned, and stood up on his chair.

'I love you. I love you all,' he said, striking a skiing pose though they all knew he could not afford the sport. 'I want to love you guys, so you better let me get the bill,' he said.

While they fought with one another to pay, the piece of paper snatched from hand to hand, Taeyeong, who was a lawyer, quietly stood up and paid for them all.

That night, after the last round of drinks at a drinking tent, Gilho returned home after 4am with Taeyeong draped over him like an overcoat. He rested his friend on the couch, then slid to the floor. It was then that he saw Wuseong on the balcony. When their eyes met, the goose tucked its hammer-shaped head underneath Wuseong's neck and made a rough, throaty sound.

Gilho slid the balcony glass door open. 'Ah-yah,' he said, 'where were you?'

Wuseong looked at him shyly; his body was

tense and guarded, as if ready to bolt.

'Were you worried?'

'Of course!' Gilho's voice shook. 'You disappear with no note, no call… it's okay. You'll be okay.'

Wuseong stood up, his arms still crossed. A goose feather stuck up from his hair.

Gilho's head thundered with confusion. He wanted the boy to know that he was sorry, but he was too proud, too afraid to admit it.

Wuseong's eyes fastened on Taeyeong, absorbed by the Hugo Boss-clad, reclining misery, as if he were another species altogether. Wuseong smiled a bright, tired smile. 'We should be going to bed.'

Gilho patted the boy on the head. He almost patted the goose before he remembered that it was just a goose. He said something about his best bottle of Bordeaux. 'I expect we'll drink to the morning.'

Snow flurries fell against the glass. Gilho returned to the kitchen and clumsily chopped at a chunk of dried squid with a steak knife. Wuseong pressed his face against the glass. On the other side, Taeyeong rubbed his eyes and breathed heavily from the sofa. All of them, strangers in their lives, watched the wintering landscape.

A shriek shattered the silence. By the time Gilho bolted back to the living room, Taeyeong, his voice dancing with fear, was gripping his bleeding hand.

Wuseong hopped nervously from left leg to right.

'Your friend kept trying to pluck her,' he said. 'I tried to stop him, I did.'

Taeyeong moaned. 'One feather – I just wanted one. To see if you can really write with one of 'em.'

Gilho headed straight for the balcony. Alcohol heightened his notion that a man should protect his friends; he was ready for a confrontation. As if it sensed his animosity, the goose trumpeted and hissed with its bill wide open; it charged, its wing billowing in the air like a stiff petticoat. Gilho grasped at the beating good wing, and felt the webbed feet on his foot. His hand seemed to reach through nothing, as if there were no body underneath the feathers. Its black pupils locked with his.

He gripped the goose's tubelike neck as best he could with both hands. It startled him to sense this immense power that one could have over life. In the haze of alcohol, he felt convinced that if this bulbous creature was extinguished with one twist, somehow his life would be simplified.

An unfamiliar shadow passed over Wuseong's face. It flickered, disappeared. He looked at Gilho as if he saw right through him, and forgave him for his cowardice.

Gilho released the goose and staggered back inside. He said, 'Why do you look at me like that?'

Taeyeong stared, his hand forgotten.

'Ajeoshi,' Wuseong said wistfully, 'the world's full of mystery – it's our duty to accept it.'

Wuseong dashed to Taeyeong's side and inspected his hand. Gilho heard him humming as if he weren't completely alone in the world; as if he weren't living with an older man cracking up with love; as if a bleak future were not awaiting him. He hummed as if hope were enough to sustain him.

An hour into sleep Gilho woke up to the first full moon of the new year. He went to the kitchen for water, then standing with the empty glass he watched car beams flashing on the nearby riverside highway, alone with the lie that he was. He no longer wanted to be different from other men. As he turned to go he heard a muffled whisper from the living room. One figure, then two, moved on the balcony. There was a woman. She was around Gilho's age with hair as black as a coffin, a body thin and frail on top, with rotund legs. She rested her head against Wuseong's shoulder. Her face was weathered with dirt and death, but her eyes were generous and untroubled, her lips were a seamless line of perseverance. The cool moonlight brightened the balcony. As the boy's hand gathered around the woman's head, her face brightened. Gilho saw her attenuated fingers, her delicate, blue-tinted feet. He saw what he had been resisting all this time: the world through Wuseong's eyes.

Gilho took a step toward the balcony, then another. When he slid open the door, Wuseong looked up, unsurprised. He slipped his hand into Gilho's.

'Isn't my mother beautiful?' Wuseong said.

Gilho nodded, afraid to say anything. He breathed in shallow bursts.

'Ajeoshi, are you all right?'

Gilho rested his hand on the boy's shoulder.

He did not care that Taeyeong might stumble out of the guest room, looking for the bathroom. It was the first full moon of the new year, Daeboreum, the day hundreds of people hiked up the mountains to catch the rising of the moon for a year's worth of luck, and bonfire festivals replayed the fires of the past that had driven away evil spirits. Tonight the apartment was Gilho's mountain where he was caught in the moon's light. He was ready to go anywhere with Wuseong. Anywhere to be far from Gilho's position, the eyes of his parents, his friends, anywhere where they could be themselves. He wanted to ask the goose for forgiveness. For wanting her son in an unforgivable way. For being a married man betraying his family. Forgiveness, because he was prepared to scandalize. Tonight he was going to kiss the boy he loved. He turned to Wuseong.

'I've been lonely,' he said, and shuddered, when the woman's arms, the goose's good, stiff feathers, circled over them. 'I've been lonely all my life.'

Black Vodka

Deborah Levy

THE FIRST TIME I met Lisa I knew she was going to help me become a very different sort of man. Knowing this felt like a summer holiday. It made me relax and I am usually quite a tense person. There is something you should know about me.

I have a hump on my back, a mound between my shoulderblades. You will notice when I wear a shirt without a jacket that there is more to me than first meets the eye. It's strange how fascinating human beings find both celebrity and deformity in their own species. People sink their eyes into my hump for six seconds longer than protocol allows, and try to work out the difference between them and myself.

The boys called me 'Ali' at school because that's what they thought camels were called. Ali Ali Ali. Ali's got the hump. The word 'playground' does not really provide an accurate sense of the sort of ethnic cleansing that went on behind the gates that were supposed to keep us safe. I was instructed in the art of Not Belonging from a very tender age. Go Ho-me Ali, Go Ho-me. In fact I was born in Southend on Sea, and so were the boys, but I was exiled to the Arabian Desert and not allowed to smoke with them behind the local cockle sheds.

There is something else you ought to know about me. I write copy for a leading advertising agency. My colleagues reluctantly respect me because they suspect I'm less content than they are. I have made it my professional business to understand that no one respects ruddy-faced happiness.

I first glimpsed Lisa at the presentation launch for the branding and naming of a new vodka. My agency had won the account for the advertising campaign and I was standing on a small raised stage, pointing to a slide of a starry night sky. I adjusted my mic clip and began.

'Black Vodka,' I said, slightly sinisterly, '... "*Vodka Noir*", will appeal to those consumers in need of stylish angst. As Victor Hugo put it so well, "We are alone, bereft and the night falls upon us." Gentlemen, to drink Black Vodka is to be in mourning for our lives.'

I explained that if vodka was mostly associated with the communist countries of the former Eastern bloc, it was well known that the exploration of abstract and subjective ideas in these regimes was the ultimate defiance of the individual against the state. Black Vodka had to hitch a nostalgic ride on all of this and be packaged as a dangerous choice for the cultured and discerning.

My colleagues sipped their lattes (the intern had just done the Starbucks run) and listened carefully to my angle. When I insisted that Vodka Noir had high cheekbones, a few of the guys laughed uneasily. I am known in the office as the Crippled Poet. And then I noticed someone sitting in the audience – a woman with long brown hair, very blonde at the ends, who was not from the agency. She had her arms folded across her grey cashmere sweater; an open notebook lay on her lap. Now and again she'd pick it up and doodle with her pencil. My sharp eyes (long sight) confirmed that this stranger in our small community was observing me rather clinically.

After my presentation my colleague Richard introduced me to the woman with the notebook. Although he did not say so, I assumed she was his new girlfriend. Richard is known for splashing his footballer's body with a heady cologne, West Indian Limes, every morning. Its effect on me is both arousing and desperately melancholy. I could buy five bottles of that seductive cologne tomorrow, yet to draw attention to my damaged body in this way would underline its difference from Richard's. Anyway, it was quite a shock to see him with the woman whose clinical gaze had for some mysterious reason awoken in me the kind of yearning for another sort of life that I was attempting to whip up in my Vodka Noir campaign.

Richard smiled affectionately at me, apparently amused at something he couldn't be bothered to explain.

'Lisa is an archaeologist. I thought she'd be interested in your presentation.'

Her eyes were long-lidded and blue.

'Would you buy Black Vodka, Lisa?'

She told me she would, yes, she would give it a go, and then she screamed because Richard had crept up behind her and his hands were clasping her narrow waist like a handcuff.

As I put away my laptop, I felt an unwelcome blast of bitter anger. I suddenly wanted more than anything else to be a man without a burden on his back. After a presentation we tend to open champagne and instruct the interns to order in snacks. But when I saw a tray of sun-dried tomatoes arranged on tiny pesto-filled pastry cases I wanted to punch them onto the floor. A lifetime spent looking forward to office canapes suddenly seemed unbearable.

I left the office early. I even left without asking my boss what he thought of my presentation. Tom Mines is the Cruel Man of the agency (though he would call his cruelty 'insight') and he suffers from livid eczema on his wrists and hands. For this reason he buys jackets with extra-long sleeves – yes, I am always fascinated by how people conceal their physical suffering. I muttered something about being summoned to an emergency and left quickly before Tom's famous 'insight' revealed the emergency was me. But I did not leave before walking straight over to Lisa, aware that Tom Mines was watching me, his thin grey fingers twisted around the cuffs of his jacket. What I did next might sound strange; I gave Richard's girlfriend my business card. The surprise she attempted to express with her facial muscles, her raised eyebrows, her mocking lips slightly parted – it really was not that convincing because of what I had seen. When Lisa was doodling in her notebook, she had let it rest open on her lap. From my position on the raised stage, I could see quite clearly that she had drawn a sketch of me on the left-hand page. A picture of a naked, hunchbacked man with every single organ of his body labelled. Underneath her rather too accurate portrait (should I be flattered that she had imagined me naked?) she'd scribbled two words: *Homo sapiens*.

She called me. Lisa actually pressed the digits that connected her voice to mine. I asked her straight away if she'd like to join me for supper that Friday. No she couldn't make Friday. It is usual for people attracted to each other to pretend they have full and busy lives, but I have an incredible facility to wade through human shame with no shoes on. I told her if she couldn't make Friday I was free on

Monday, Tuesday, Wednesday and Thursday, and that the weekend looked hopeful too.

We agreed to meet on Wednesday in South Kensington (she said she liked the big sky in that part of town) and I suggested we drink our way through the vast menu of flavoured vodkas at the Polish Club, not far from the Royal Albert Hall. This way we could conduct a bit of field research for my Vodka Noir concept. She said she was more than happy to be my assistant. That night I went to bed and dreamt (again) of Poland. In this recurring dream I am in Warsaw on a train to Southend on Sea. There is a soldier in my carriage. He kisses his mother's hand and then he kisses his girlfriend's lips. I am watching him in the old mirror attached to the wall of our carriage and I can see he has a humped back under his khaki uniform. When I wake up there are always tears on my cheeks, transparent as vodka but warm as rain.

There's something about rain that makes me slam the doors of cabs extra hard. I love the rain. It heightens every gesture, injects it with 5 ml of unspecific yearning. On Wednesday night it was raining when the cab dropped me off on Exhibition Road in London's Zone 1. In the distance I could see autumn leaves on the tall trees in Hyde Park. The air was soft and cool. I began to walk up Exhibition Road and knew that where now there are paving stones there were once fields and market gardens. I wanted to lie in one of those ancient London fields with Lisa stretched lazily across my lap, and I wanted the schoolboys who told me I was a freak to watch us as we murmured in the grass, the clouds unfolding above us.

I walked deliberately slowly to the white Georgian town house that is the Polish Club. The building was donated to the Polish resistance during the Second World War and later became a cultural meeting place, a second home to the refugees and exiles who could not return to a Stalin-shaped Poland. As you might guess, I have made it my business to study the deformities of famous and powerful men. Like myself, Stalin was physically misshapen; his face was pitted from the smallpox that he had contracted as a child, one of his arms was longer than the other, his eyes were yellow (people called him 'tiger') and he was short enough in stature to wear platform shoes.

I have never worn shoes with heels to make me feel bolder, but I have always felt like lost property, someone waiting to be claimed. To be offered an elegant home for a few hours at the hospitable Polish Club always does good things for my dignity.

I hung my coat on a wooden hanger, placed it on the clothes rail in the foyer and made my way into the bar, where my booking in the dining room was confirmed by a polite and serene waitress from Lublin. She discreetly invited me to 'enjoy a drink until my companion arrives.'

Tragically keen to obey her, I ordered an extra shot of pepper vodka. Thirty minutes later I had researched the raspberry, peppermint, honey, caraway, plum and apple vodkas and my companion had still not arrived. The sky was darkening outside the window. An elderly woman in a green felt hat sat on the velvet chair next to me, scribbling some sort of mathematical equation on a scrap of paper. She was so lost in thought that I began to worry that somewhere else in the world, another mathematician would pick up on those thoughts and at this very moment, 8.25pm, find a strategy to solve the equation before she did. It was possible that while she sat in her chair struggling with the endless zeros that seemed to deeply perplex her, someone else would be standing on a stage in Brazil or Ljubljana collecting a fat cheque for their contribution to human knowledge. Would I, too, be waiting in endless humiliation for Lisa, who was probably at this moment lying in Richard's arms while he kissed the zero of her mouth?

No I would not. She arrived, late and breathless and I could see she was genuinely sorry to have kept me waiting. I ordered her three shot glasses of the cherry vodka while she told me the reason she was late was that she had been planning a dig that was soon to take place in Cornwall, but the computer had crashed and she'd lost most of her data.

There is nothing that feels as good as living in the present tense if you are breathing near someone you desire. This is where I want to live, in the here and now of The Polish Club forever; the past of my youth was not a good place to be. Is it strange, then, that I am attracted to a woman who is mostly concerned with digging up the past? Lisa and I are sitting in the dining room on our first date. We arrange the starched linen napkins over our laps and nervously discuss the oily black eggs, the caviar that comes from the beluga, osetra and sevruga varieties of sturgeon. The waitress from Lublin takes our order and Lisa, naturally, wants to know less about fish and more about me.

'So where do you live?' She asks me this as if I am an exotic find she is required to label in black Indian ink.

I tell her I own a three-bedroomed flat with a west-facing balcony in a Victorian double-fronted villa in Notting Hill Gate. I want to bore her.

I tell her I never dream or cry or swear or shake or snack on cereal instead of apples. Better slowly to prove more interesting than I first appear.

Lisa looks bored.

I tell that my mother wanted me to be a priest because she thought I'd look best in loose fitting clothes.

She laughs and plays with the ends of her hair. She shuts her eyes and then opens them. She fiddles with her mobile - the modern umbilicus that adults need to hang on to in order to convince themselves they are not bereft and alone in the world.

Lisa shuffles her shoes, which are red and suede. She eats a hearty portion of duck with apple sauce and discovers I like delicate dumplings stuffed with mushroom because I am a vegetarian. When she stabs her fork into the meat it oozes pale red blood, which she mops up with a piece of white bread; little delicate dabs of the wrist as she brings the blood and bread up to her mouth. She eats with appetite and enjoyment. That she is a carnivore pleases me. After a while she orders a slice of cheesecake and asks me if I was born a hunchback.

'Yes.'

'Sometimes it's difficult to tell.'

'What do you mean?'

'Well, some people have bad posture.'

'Oh.'

Lisa licks her fingers. Apparently it's an excellent cheesecake; I am pleased she is pleased. The waitress offers us a glass of liqueur from a bottle that has 'a whole Italian pear' lurking inside it. The pear is peeled. It is a naked pear. We accept, and I say to Lisa, 'We should get that pear out of the bottle and make a sorbet with it' – as if that is something I do all the time. She likes that. It is as if the invitation to wedge the pear out of the bottle is like freeing a genie. She becomes more animated and talks about her job. Apparently what most interests her is the human form. When she finds human remains on a dig – bones, for example – they have to be stored in a methodical way. Heavy bones, the long bones, are packed at the bottom of a box, while lighter bones such as vertebrae are packed at the top.

'Archaeology is an approach to uncovering the past,' she tells me, sipping her liqueur, which strangely does not taste of pear.

'So when you go on a dig you record and interpret the physical remains of the past, is that right?'

'Sort of. I like to know how people used to live and what their habits were.'

'You dig up their beliefs and culture.'

'Well, you can't dig up a belief,' she says. 'But the material culture, the objects and artefacts that people leave behind, will give me clues to their beliefs.'

'I see. You know why I like you, Lisa?'

'Why do you like me?'

'Because I think you see me as an archaeological site.'

'I am a bit of an explorer,' she says. 'I'd like to see the bone that protrudes in your thoracic spine.'

At that moment I drop the silver fork in my right hand. It falls noiselessly to the carpet and bounces before it falls again. I bend down to pick it up, and because I am nervous and have downed too many vodkas, I start to go on an archaeological dig of my own. In my mind I lift up the faded rose-pink carpet of the Polish Hearth Club in South Kensington and find underneath it a forest full of wild mushrooms and swooping bats that live upside down. This is a Polish forest covered in new snow in the murderous twentieth century. A grey wolf shelters under a pine tree. At the same time, in the twenty-first, I can see the feet of customers eating herrings with sour cream two metres away from my own table. Their shoes are made from suede and leather. When the wolf starts to dig up an unnamed grave that has just been filled with soil, I'm frightened by the dark forest in my mind, so I pick up the fork and glance at Lisa, who has been gazing at the lump on my back as if staring through the lens of a microscope.

The rain tonight is horizontal. It makes me feel reckless. I want to give in to its force. As we walk onto Exhibition Road I slip my arm around Lisa's shoulders and she does not grimace. Her hair is soaking wet and so are her red suede shoes.

'I am going home,' she tells me. She hails a vacant taxi on the other side of the road, and all the time the warm rain falls upon us like the tears in my dream. Her voice is gentle. Rain does that to voices. It makes them intimate and suggestive. While the taxi does a U-turn she stands behind me and presses her hands into my hump as if she is listening to it breathe. And then she takes her forefinger and traces around it, getting an exact sense of its shape. It's the kind of thing cops do to a corpse with a piece of chalk. Now Lisa bends down and opens the door of the taxi. As she slides her long legs into the back seat, she shouts her destination to the driver. 'Tower Bridge.'

He nods and adjusts the meter.

When she smiles I can see her sharp white teeth.

'Look, you know that Richard is my boyfriend – but why don't you come home with me to compare notes on vodka?'

I don't need any persuading. I jump in beside her and slam the door extra hard. As the cab pulls out, Lisa leans forwards and starts to kiss me. Does she want to know more about my habits and beliefs and how I live? Or is she curious to find out if her sketch of *Homo sapiens* was an accurate representation of my body?

The meter is going berserk like my heartbeat while the moon drifts over the Natural History Museum. Somewhere inside it, pressed under glass, are twelve ghost moths (*Hepialus humuli*), of earliest evolutionary lineage. These ghosts once flew in pastures, dropped their eggs to the ground and slept through the day. There is so much of life to record and classify it's hard to know what kind of language to find for it, so I will start exactly where I am now. Life is beautiful! Vodka is black! Pears are naked! Rain is horizontal! Moths are ghosts! Only some of this is true, but you should know this does not scare me as much as the promise of love.

East of the West

Miroslav Penkov

It takes me thirty years, and the loss of those I love, to finally arrive in Beograd. Now I'm pacing outside my cousin's apartment, flowers in one hand and a bar of chocolate in the other, rehearsing the simple question I want to ask her. A moment ago, a Serbian cab driver spat on me and I take time to wipe the spot on my shirt. I count to eleven.

'Vera,' I repeat once more in my head, 'will you marry me?'

★

I first met Vera in the summer of 1970, when I was six. At that time my folks and I lived on the Bulgarian side of the river, in the village of Bulgarsko Selo, while she and her folks made their home on the other bank, in Srbsko. A long time ago these two villages had been one – that of Staro Selo – but after the great wars Bulgaria had lost land and that land had been given to the Serbs. The river, splitting the village into two hamlets, had served as a boundary – what lay east of the river stayed in Bulgaria and what lay west belonged to Serbia.

Because of the unusual predicament the two villages were in, our people had managed to secure permission from both countries to hold, once every five years, a major reunion, called the sbor. This was done officially so we wouldn't forget our roots. In reality, though, the reunion was just another excuse for everyone to eat lots of grilled meat and drink lots of rakia. A man had to eat until he felt sick from eating, drink until he no longer cared if he felt sick from eating. The summer of 1970, the reunion was going to be in Srbsko, which meant we had to cross the river first.

This is how we cross:

Booming noise and balls of smoke above the water. Mihalaky is coming down the river on his boat. The boat is glorious. Not a boat really, but a raft with a motor. Mihalaky has taken the seat of an old Moskvich, the Russian car with the engine of a tank, and he has nailed that seat to the floor of the raft and upholstered the seat with goat skin. Hair out. Black and white spots, with brown. He sits on his throne, calm, terrible. He sucks on a pipe with an ebony mouthpiece and his long white hair flows behind him like a flag.

On the banks are our people. Waiting. Father holds a white lamb under one arm and on his shoulder he balances a demijohn of grape rakia.

His shining eyes are fixed on the boat. He licks his lips. Beside him rests a wooden cask, stuffed with white cheese. My uncle sits on the cask, counts Bulgarian money.

'I hope they have Deutsche Marks to sell,' he says.

'They always do,' my father tells him.

Mother is behind them, holding two sacks. One is full of terlitsi – booties she has been knitting for months, gifts for our folks on the other side. The second is zipped up and I can't see what's inside, but I know. Flasks of rose oil, lipstick, and mascara. She will sell them or trade them for other perfumes or lipsticks or mascara. Next to her is my sister, Elitsa, pressing to her chest a small teddy bear stuffed with money. She's been saving. She wants to buy jeans.

'Levis,' she says. 'Like the rock star.'

My sister knows a lot about the West.

I'm standing between Grandma and Grandpa. Grandma is wearing her most beautiful costume – a traditional dress she got from her own Grandma, that she will one day give to my sister. Motley-patterned apron, white hemp shirt, embroidery. On her ears, her most precious ornament – the silver earrings.

Grandpa is twisting his moustache.

'The little bastard,' he's saying, 'he better pay now.'

He is referring to his cousin, uncle Radko, who owes him money on account of a football bet.

Uncle Radko had taken his sheep by the cliffs, where the river narrowed, and seeing Grandpa herding his animals on the opposite bluff, shouted, *I bet your Bulgars will lose in London*, and Grandpa shouted back, *You wanna put some money on it?* And that's how the bet was made, thirty years ago.

There are nearly a hundred of us on the bank and it takes Mihalaky a day to get us all across the river. No customs – the men pay something to the guards and all is good. When the last person sets his foot in Srbsko, the moon is bright in the sky and the air smells of grilled pork and foaming wine.

Eating, drinking, dancing. All night long. In the morning everyone has passed out in the meadow. There are only two souls not drunk or sleeping. One of them is me and the other one, going through the pockets of my folks, is my cousin Vera.

Two things I found remarkable about my cousin: her jeans and her sneakers. Aside from that she was a scrawny girl – a pale, round face and fragile shoulders with skin peeling from the sun. Her hair was long, or was it my sister's hair that grew down to her waist? I forget. But I do recall the first thing that my cousin ever said to me:

'Let go of my hair,' she said, 'or I'll punch you in the mouth.'

I didn't because I had to stop her from stealing, so, as promised, she punched me. Only she wasn't very accurate and her fist landed on my nose, crushing it like a Plain Biscuit. I spent the rest of the sbor with tape on my face, sneezing blood, and now I am forever marked with an ugly snoot. Which is why everyone, except my mother, calls me Nose.

★

Five summers slipped by. I went to school in the village and in the afternoons I helped Father with the fields. Father drove an MTZ-50, a tractor made in Minsk. He'd put me on his lap and make me hold the steering wheel and the steering wheel would shake and twitch in my hands, as the tractor ploughed diagonally leaving terribly distorted lines behind.

'My arms hurt,' I'd say, 'this wheel is too hard.'

'Nose,' Father would say, 'quit whining. You're not holding a wheel. You're holding Life by the throat. So get your shit together and learn how to choke the bastard, because the bastard already knows how to choke you.'

Mother worked as a teacher in the school, which was awkward, because I couldn't call her 'Mother' in class and because she always knew if I hadn't done my homework. But I had access to her files and could steal exams and sell them to the kids for cash.

The year of the new sbor, 1975, our geography teacher retired and Mother found herself teaching his classes as well. This gave me more exams to sell and I made good money. I had a goal in mind. I went to my sister Elitsa, having first rubbed my eyes hard so they would appear filled with tears, and with my most humble voice I asked to buy her jeans.

'Nose,' she said, 'I love you, but I'll wear these jeans until the day I die.'

I tried to look heartbroken, but she didn't budge. She told me to ask cousin Vera for a pair and pay her at the sbor. Then from a jar in her night stand she took out ten levs and stuffed them in my pocket. 'Get something nice,' she said.

Two months before it was time for the reunion I went to the river. I yelled until a boy showed up and I asked him to call my cousin. She came an hour later.

'What do you want?'

'Levis,' I yelled.

'You better have the money,' she yelled back.

Mihalaky came in smoke and roar. And with him came the West. My cousin Vera stepped out of the boat and everything on her screamed *We live better than you, we have more stuff, stuff you can't have and never will*. She wore white leather shoes with a little flower on them, which she explained was called an Adidas. She had jeans. And her shirt said things in English.

'What does it say?'

'The name of a music group. They have this song that goes "*Smooook na dar voooto.*" You heard it?'

'Of course I have.' But she knew better.

After lunch, the grown-ups danced around the fire, then played drunk football. Elitsa was absent for most of the time, and finally when she returned, her lips were burning red and her eyes shone like I'd never seen them before. She pulled me aside and whispered in my ear:

'Promise not to tell.' Then she pointed at a dark-haired boy from Srbsko, skinny and with a long neck, who was just joining the match. 'Boban and I kissed in the forest. It was so great,' and her voice flickered. She nudged me in the ribs, and stuck a finger at cousin Vera, who sat by the fire, yawning and raking the embers up with a stick.

'Come on, Nose, be a man. Take her to the woods.'

And she laughed so loud even the deaf old grandmas turned to look at us.

I scurried away, disgusted, ashamed, but finally I had to approach Vera. I asked if she had my jeans, then took out the money and began to count it.

'Not here, you fool,' she said and slapped my hand with the smoldering stick.

We walked through the village until we reached the old bridge, which stood solitary in the middle of the road. Yellow grass grew between each stone, and the riverbed was dry and fissured.

We hid under the bridge and completed the swap. Thirty levs for a pair of jeans. Best deal I'd ever made.

'Wanna go for a walk?' Vera said after

counting the bills twice. She rubbed them on her face, the way our fathers did, and shoved them in her pocket.

We picked mushrooms in the woods, while she told me school stories, and complained about a Serbian boy who always pestered her.

'I can teach him a lesson,' I said. 'Next time I come there you show him to me.'

'Yeah, Nose, like you can fight.'

And then just like that, she hit me in the nose. Crushed it, once more, like a biscuit.

'Why did you do that?'

She shrugged. I made a fist to smack her back, but how do you hit a girl? Or how, for that matter, will hitting another person in the face stop the blood gushing from your own nose? I tried to suck it up and act like the pain was easy to ignore.

She took me by the hand and dragged me toward the river.

'I like you, Nose,' she said. 'Let's go wash your face.'

We lay on the banks and chewed thyme leaves.

'Nose,' my cousin said, 'you know what they told us in school?'

She rolled over and I did the same. Her eyes were dark, shaped like apricot kernels. Her face was all speckled and she had a tiny spot on her upper lip, delicate, hard to notice, that got redder when she was nervous or angry. The spot was red now.

'You look like a mouse,' I told her.

She rolled her eyes.

'Our history teacher,' she said, 'told us we were all Serbs. A hundred percent.'

'Well, you talk funny,' I said. 'Serbianish.'

'So you think I'm a Serb?'

'Where do you live?' I asked her.

'You know where.'

'But do you live in Serbia or in Bulgaria?'

Her eyes darkened and she held them shut for a long time. I knew she was sad. And I liked it. She had nice shoes, and jeans, and could listen to bands from the West, but I owned something that had been taken away from her forever.

'The only Bulgarian here is me,' I told her.

She got up and stared at the river. 'Let's swim to the drowned church,' she said.

'I don't want to get shot.'

'Get shot? Who cares for churches in no man's water? Besides, I've swum there before.' She took her shirt off and jumped in. The murky current rippled around her shoulders and they glistened, smooth, round pebbles the river had polished for ages. Yet, her skin was soft, I could imagine. I almost reached to touch it.

We swam the river slowly, staying along the bank. I caught a small chub under a rock, but Vera made me let it go. Finally we saw the cross sticking up above the water, massive, with rusty feet and arms that caught the evening sun.

We all knew well the story of the drowned

church. Back in the day, before the Balkan Wars, a rich man lived east of the river. He had no offspring and no wife, so when he lay down dying he called his servant with a final wish – to build, with his money, a village church. The church was built, west of the river, and the peasants hired from afar a young zograf, a master of icons. The master painted for two years and there he met a girl and fell in love with her and married her and they too lived west of the river, near the church.

Then came the Balkan Wars and after that the First World War. All these wars Bulgaria lost, and much Bulgarian land was given to the Serbs. Three officials arrived in the village; one was a Russian, one was French, and one was British. East of the river, they said, stays in Bulgaria. West of the river from now on belongs to Serbia. Soldiers guarded the banks and planned to take the bridge down, and when the young master, who had gone away to work on another church, came back, the soldiers refused to let him cross the border and return to his wife.

In his desperation he gathered people and convinced them to divert the river, to push it west until it went around the village. Because according to the orders, what lay east of the river stayed in Bulgaria.

How they carried all those stones, all those logs, how they piled them up I cannot imagine. Why the soldiers didn't stop them I don't know. The river moved west and it looked like she would serpent around the village. But then she twisted, wiggled and tasted with her tongue a route of lesser resistance – through the lower hamlet she swept, devouring people and houses. Even the church, in which the master had left two years of his life, was lost in her belly.

We stared at the cross for some time, then I got out on the bank and sat in the sun.

'It's pretty deep,' I said. 'You sure you've been down there?'

She put a hand on my back. 'It's okay if you're scared.'

But it wasn't okay. I closed my eyes, took a deep breath, and dove off the bank.

'Swim to the cross,' she yelled after me.

I swam like I wore shoes of iron. I held the cross tightly and stepped on the slimy dome underneath. Soon Vera stood by me, in turn gripping the cross so she wouldn't drift away.

'Let's look at the walls,' she said.

'What if we get stuck?'

'Then we'll drown.'

She laughed and nudged me in the chest.

'Come on, Nose, do it for me.'

It was difficult to keep my eyes open at first. The current pushed us away so we had to work hard to reach the small window below the dome. We grabbed the bars on the window and looked inside. And despite the murky water, my eyes fell on a painting of a bearded man kneeling by a rock, his hands entwined. The man was looking down and in the distance, approaching, was a little bird. Below the bird, I saw a cup.

'It's a nice church,' Vera said after we surfaced.

'Want to dive again?'

'No.' She moved closer and quickly kissed me on the lips.

'Why did you do that?' I said, and felt the hairs on my arms and neck stand up, though they were wet.

She shrugged, then pushed herself off the dome, and laughing, swam splashing up the river.

★

The jeans Vera sold me that summer were about two sizes too large, and it seemed like they'd been worn before, but that didn't bother me. I even slept in them. I liked how loose they were around my waist, how much space, how much Western freedom they provided around my legs.

But for my sister Elitsa, life worsened. The West gave her ideas. She often went to the river and sat on the bank and stared, quietly, for hours on end. She sighed and her bony shoulders dropped, like the earth below her was pulling on her arms.

As the weeks went by, her face lost its plumpness. Her skin got greyer, her eyes muddier. At dinner she kept her head down, and played with her food. She never spoke, not to Mother, not to me. She was as quiet as a painting on a wall.

A doctor came and left puzzled. 'I leave

puzzled,' he said. 'She's healthy. I just don't know what's wrong with her.'

But I knew. That longing in my sister's eyes, that disappointment, I'd seen them in Vera's eyes before, on the day she had wished to be Bulgarian. It was the same look of defeat, scary and contagious, and because of that look, I kept my distance.

★

I didn't see Vera for a year. Then one summer day in 1976 as I was washing my jeans in the river, she yelled from the other side.

'Nose, you're buck naked.'

That was supposed to embarrass me, but I didn't even twitch.

'I like to rub my ass in the face of the West,' I yelled back and raised the jeans, dripping with soap.

'What?' she yelled.

'I like to…' I waved. 'What do you want?'

'Nose, I got something for you. Wait for – and – to – church.'

'What?'

'Wait for the dark. And swim.'

'You gonna be there?'

'What?'

I didn't bother. I waved, bent over and went on washing my jeans.

I waited for my folks to go to sleep, then snuck out the window. The lights in my sister's room were still on and I imagined her in bed, eyes tragically fixed on the ceiling.

I hid my clothes under a bush and stepped into the cool water. On the other side I could see the guard's flashlight, the tip of his cigarette, red in the dark. I swam slowly, as quietly as I could. In places the river flowed so narrow people could stand on both sides and talk and almost hear each other, but around the drowned church the river was broad, a quarter mile between the banks.

I stepped on the algae-slick dome and ran my fingers along a string tied to the base of the cross. A nylon bag was fixed to the other end. I freed the bag and was ready to glide away when someone said, 'I hope you like them.'

Vera swam closer, and was suddenly locked in a circle of light.

The guard shouted something and his dog barked.

'Go, you stupid,' Vera said and splashed away. The circle of light followed.

I held the cross tight, without a sound. I knew this was no joke. The guards shot trespassers if they had to. But Vera swam unhurriedly.

'Faster,' the guard shouted. 'Get out here.'

The beam of light etched her naked body in the night. She had the breasts of a woman.

He asked her something and she spoke back. Then he slapped her. He held her very close and felt her body. She kneed him in the groin. He laughed on the ground long after she'd run away naked.

All through, of course, I watched in silence. I could have yelled something to stop him, but then, he had a gun. And so I held the cross and so the river flowed black with night around me and even out on the bank I felt sticky with dirty water.

Inside the bag were Vera's old Adidas. The laces were in bad shape, and the left shoe was a bit torn at the front, but they were still excellent. And suddenly all shame was gone and my heart pounded so hard with new excitement, I was afraid the guards might hear it. On the bank I put the shoes on and they fit perfectly. Well, they were a bit too small for my feet, actually, they were really quite tight, but they were worth the pain. I didn't walk. I swam across the air.

I was striding back home, when someone giggled in the bush. Grass rustled. I hesitated, but snuck through the dark and I saw two people rolling on the ground, and would have watched them in secret if it wasn't for the squelching shoes.

'Nose, is that you?' a girl asked. She flinched, and tried to cover herself with a shirt, but this was the night I saw my second pair of breasts. These belonged to my sister.

I lay in my room, head under the blanket, trying to make sense of what I'd seen, when someone walked in.

'Are you sleeping?'

My sister sat on the bed and put her hand on my chest.

'Come on. I know you're awake.'

I asked her what she wanted and threw the blanket off. I could not see her face for the dark, but I could feel that gaze of hers. The house was quiet. Only Father snored in the other room.

'Are you going to tell them?' she said.

'No. What you do is your own business.'

She leaned forward and kissed me on the forehead.

'You smell like cigarettes,' I said. 'Goodnight, Nose.'

She got up to leave, but I pulled her down.

'Elitsa, what are you ashamed of? Why don't you tell them?'

'Boban's from Srbsko.'

I sat up in my bed and took her cold hand.

'What are you gonna do?' I asked her. She shrugged.

'I want to run away with him,' she said and her voice became, suddenly softer, though what she spoke of scared me deeply. 'We're going to go West. Get married, have kids. I want to work as a hair-stylist in Munich. Boban has a cousin there. A hair-stylist, or she washes dogs or something.' She ran her fingers through my hair. 'Oh, Nose,' she said. 'Tell me what to do.'

★

I couldn't tell her. And so she kept living unhappy, wanting to be with that boy day and night but seeing him rarely and in secret. 'I am alive,' she told me, 'only when I'm with him.' And then she spoke of their plans, hitchhiking to Munich, staying with Boban's cousin and helping her cut hair. 'It's a sure thing, Nose,' she'd say and I believed her.

It was the spring of 1980 when Josip Tito died and even I knew things were about to change in Yugoslavia. The old men in our village whispered that now, with the Yugoslav president finally planted in a mausoleum, our western neighbour would fall apart. I pictured in my mind the aberration I'd seen in a film, a monster sewn together from the legs and arms and torso of different people. I pictured someone pulling on the thread that held these body parts, the thread unravelling, until the legs and arms and torso came undone. We could snatch a finger then, the land across the river, and patch it up back to our land. That's what the old folks spoke about, drinking their rakia in the tavern. Meanwhile, the young folks escaped to the city, following new jobs. There weren't enough children in the village anymore to justify our own school and so we started studying in another village, with other kids. Mother lost her job. Grandpa got sick with pneumonia, but Grandma gave him herbs for a month, and he got better. Mostly. Father worked two jobs, then stacked hay on the weekends. He had no time to take me ploughing.

But Vera and I saw each other often, sometimes twice a month. I never found the courage to speak of the soldier. At night, we swam to the drowned church and played around the cross, very quiet, like river rats. And there, by the cross we kissed our first real kiss. Was it joy I felt? Or was it sadness? To hold her so close and taste her breath, her lips, to slide a finger down her shoulder. To lay my palm upon her breasts and know that someone else had done this, with force, while I had watched, tongue swallowed. Her face was silver with moonlight, her hair dripped dark with dark water.

'Do you love me?' she said.

'Yes,' I said. I said, 'I wish we never had to leave the water.'

'You fool,' she said and kissed me again. 'People can't live in rivers.'

★

That June, two months before the new sbor, our parents found out about Boban. One evening, when I came home for supper, I discovered the whole family in the yard, under the trellis. The village priest was there. The village doctor. Elitsa was weeping, her face aflame. The priest made her kiss an iron cross and sprinkled her with holy water from an enormous copper. The doctor buckled his bag, winked at me and made for the gate. On his way out, the priest gave my forehead a thrashing with the boxwood foliage.

'What's the matter?' I said, dripping holy water.

Grandpa shook his head. Mother put her hand on my sister's. 'You've had your cry,' she said.

'Father,' I said, 'why was the doctor winking? And why did the priest bring such a giant copper?'

Father looked at me, furious. 'Because your sister, Nose,' he said, 'requires an Olympic pool to cleanse her.'

'Meaning?' I said.

'Meaning,' he said, 'your sister is pregnant. Meaning,' he said, 'we'll have to get her married.'

My family, dressed up, went to the river. On the other bank Boban's family already waited for us. Mother had washed my collar with sugar water to stiffen it, and I could feel the sugar running down my back in a syrupy stream. I tried to scratch the itch, but Grandpa told me to quit fidgeting and be a man. My back got itchier.

From the other side, Boban's father shouted, 'We want your daughter's hand.'

Father took out a flask and drank rakia, then passed it around. The drink tasted bad and set my throat on fire. I coughed and Grandpa smacked my back, and shook his head. Father took the flask from me and spilled some liquor on the ground for the departed. The family on the other side did the same.

'I give you my daughter's hand,' Father yelled. 'We'll wed them at the sbor.'

Elitsa's wedding was going to be the culmination of the sbor, so everyone prepared. Vera told me that with special permission Mihalaky had transported seven calves across the river, and two had already been slain for jerky. The two of us met often, secretly, by the drowned church.

One evening, after dinner, my family gathered under the trellis. The grownups smoked and talked of the wedding. My sister and I listened, smiled when our eyes met.

'Elitsa,' Grandma said and lay a thick bundle on the table. 'This is yours now.'

My sister untied the bundle and her eyes teared up when she recognised Grandma's best costume readied for the wedding. They lay each part of the dress on its own – the white hemp shirt, the motley apron, the linen gown, festoons of coins, the intricately worked silver earrings. Elitsa lifted the gown, and felt the linen between her fingers, and then began to put it on.

'My God, child,' Mother said, 'take your jeans off.'

Without shame, for we were all blood, Elitsa folded her jeans aside and carefully slipped inside the glowing gown. Mother helped her with the shirt. Grandpa strapped on the apron, and Father, with his fingers shaking, gently put on her ears the silver earrings.

I woke up in the middle of the night, because I'd heard a dog howl in my sleep. When I went to the kitchen to get a drink of water I saw Elitsa, ready to sneak out.

'What are you doing?' I said.

'Quiet, dechko. I'll be back in no time.'

'Are you going out to see him?'

'I want to show him these.' She dangled the earrings in her hand.

'And if they catch you?'

She put a finger to her lips, then spun on her heel. Her jeans rasped softly and she sank into the dark. I was this close to waking up Father, but how can you judge others when love is involved? I trusted she knew what she was doing.

For a long time I remembered the howling dog in my dream. And then from the river, a machine gun rattled. The guard dogs barked, the village dogs answered. I lay in bed petrified, and didn't move even when someone banged on the gates.

My sister never swam to the Serbian side. Boban always came to meet her on our bank. But that night, strangely, they had decided to meet in Srbsko one last time before the wedding. A soldier in training had seen her climb out of the river. He'd told them both to stop. Two bullets had gone through Elitsa's back when she had tried to run.

This moment in my life I do not want to remember again:

Mihalaky in smoke and roar is coming up the river, and on his boat lies my sister.

★

There was no sbor that year. There were, instead, two funerals. We dressed Elitsa in her wedding costume and lay her beautiful in a terrible coffin. The silver earrings were not beside her.

The village gathered on our side of the river. On the other side was the other village, burying their boy. I could see the grave they'd dug, same depth, same earth.

There were three priests on our side, because Grandma wouldn't accept any communist godlessness. Each of us held a candle, and the people across from us also held candles, and the banks came alive with fire, two hands of fire that could not come together. Between those hands was the river.

The first priest began to sing, and both sides listened. My eyes were on Elitsa. I couldn't let her go and things misted in my head.

'One generation passes away,' I thought the priest was singing, 'and another comes: but the earth remains forever. The sun rises and the sun goes down, and hastens to the place where it rises. The wind goes toward the West, toward Serbia, and all the rivers run away, East of the West. What has been is what will be, and what has been done is what will be done. Nothing is new under the sun.'

The voice of the priest died down, then a priest on the other side sang. The words piled on my heart like stones and I thought how much I wanted to be like the river, which had no memory, and how little like the earth, which could never forget.

★

Mother quit the factory and locked herself home. She said her hands burned with her daughter's blood. Father began to frequent the cooperative distillery at the end of the village. At first he claimed that assisting people with loading their plums, peaches, grapes into the cauldrons kept his mind blank; then that he was only sampling the first rakia which trickled out the spout, so he could advise the folk how to boil better drink.

He lost both his jobs, and so it was up to me to feed the family. I started working in the coal mine, because the money was good, and because I wanted, with my pick, to gut the land we walked on.

The control across the borders tightened. Both countries put nets along the banks and blocked buffer zones at the narrow waist of the river where the villagers used to call to one another. The sbors were cancelled. Vera and I no longer met, though we found two small hills we could sort of see each other from, like dots in the distance. But these hills were too far away and we did not go there often.

Almost every night, I dreamed of Elitsa.

'I saw her just before she left,' I would tell Mother. 'I could have stopped her.'

'Then why didn't you?' Mother would ask.

Sometimes I went to the river and threw stones over the fence, into the water, and imagined those two silver earrings, settling into the silty bottom.

'Give back the earrings,' I'd scream, 'you spineless, muddy thief.'

★

I worked double shifts in the mine and was able to put something aside. I took care of Mother who never left her bed, and occasionally brought bread and cheese to Father at the distillers. 'Mother is sick,' I'd tell him, but he pretended not to hear. 'More heat,' he'd call, and kneel by the trickle to sample some parvak.

Vera and I wrote letters for a while, but after each letter there was a longer period of silence before the new one arrived. One day, in the summer of 1990, I received a brief note:

Dear Nose. I'm getting married. I want you at my wedding. I live in Beograd now. I'm sending you money. Please come.

There was, of course, no money in the envelope. Someone had stolen it on the way.

Each day I reread the letter, and thought of the way Vera had written those words, in her elegant writing, and thought of this man she'd fallen in love with, and I wondered if she loved him as much as she'd loved me, by the cross, in the river. I made plans to get a passport.

★

Two weeks before the wedding, Mother died. The

doctor couldn't tell us of what. Of grief, the wailers said, and threw their black kerchiefs over their heads like ash. Father brought his drinking guiltily to the empty house. One day he poured me a glass of rakia and made me gulp it down. We killed the bottle. Then he grabbed my hand. Poor soul, he thought he was squeezing it hard.

'I want to see the fields,' he said.

We staggered out of the village, finishing a second bottle. When we reached the fields we sat down, and watched in silence. After the fall of communism, organized agriculture had died in many areas, and now everything was overgrown with thornbush and nettles.

'What happened, Nose?' Father said. 'I thought we held him good, this bastard, in both hands. Remember what I taught you? Hold tight, choke the bastard and things will be alright? Well, shit, Nose. I was wrong.'

And he spat against the wind, in his own face.

★

Three years passed before Vera wrote again. *Nose, I have a son. I'm sending you a picture. His name is Vladislav. Guess who we named him after? Come visit us. We have money now, so don't worry. Goran just got back from a mission in Kosovo. Can you come?*

My father wanted to see the picture. He stared at it for a long time, and his eyes watered.

'My God, Nose,' he said. 'I can't see anything. I've finally gone blind.'

'Should I call the doctor?'

'Yes,' he said, 'but for yourself. Quit the mine, or that cough will take you.'

'And money?'

'You'll find some for my funeral. Then you'll go away.'

I sat by his side and lay a hand on his forehead. 'You're burning. I'll call the doctor.'

'Nose,' he said, 'I've finally figured it out. Here is my paternal advice: go away. You can't have a life here. You must forget about your sister, about your mother, about me. Go west. Get a job in Spain, or Germany, or anywhere, start from scratch. Break each chain. This land is a bitch and you can't expect anything good from a bitch.'

He kissed my hand.

'Go get the priest,' he said.

★

I worked the mine until, in the spring of 1995, my boss, who'd come from some big, important city to the East, asked me, three times in a row, to repeat my request for an extra shift. Three times I repeated before he threw his arms up in despair. 'I can't understand your dialect, mayna,' he said. 'Too Serbian for me.' So I beat him up and was fired.

After that, I spent my days in the village tavern, every now and then lifting my hand before my eyes to check if I hadn't finally gone blind. It's a tough lot to be last in your bloodline. I thought of my father's advice, which seemed foolish, of my sister making plans to go west and of how I had done nothing to stop her from swimming to her death.

Almost every night I had the same dream. I was diving at the drowned church, looking through its window, at walls no longer covered with the murals of saints and martyrs. Instead, I could see my sister and my mother, my father, Grandpa, Grandma, Vera, people from our village, and from the village across the border, painted motionless on the walls, with their eyes on my face. And every time as I tried to push up to the surface, I discovered that my hands were locked together on the other side of the bars.

I would wake up with a yell, the voice of my sister echoing in the room.

'I have some doubts,' she would say, *'some suspicions, that these earrings aren't really silver.'*

★

In the spring of 1999 the United States attacked Serbia. Kosovo, the field where the Serb had once, many centuries ago, surrendered to the Turk, had once again become the ground of battle. Three or four times I saw American planes swoop over our village with a boom. Serbia, it seemed, was land not large enough for their manoeuvres at ultrasonic speed. They cut corners from our sky and went back to drop their bombs on our neighbours. The news that Vera's husband was killed came as no surprise. Her letter ended like this: *Nose, I have my son and you. Please come. There is no one else.*

The day I received the letter I swam to the drowned church, without taking my shoes or my clothes off. I held the cross and shivered for a long time, and finally I dove down and down to the rocky bottom. I gripped the bars on the church gates tightly and listened to the screaming of my lungs, while they squeezed out every molecule of oxygen. I wish I could say that I saw my life unwinding thread by thread before my eyes, happy moments alternating with sad, or that my sister, bathed in glorious light, came out of the church to take my drowning hand. But there was only darkness, booming of water, of blood.

Yes, I am a coward. I have an ugly nose, and the heart of a mouse, and the only drowning I can do is in a bottle of rakia. I swam out, and lay on the bank. And as I breathed with new thirst, a boom shook the air, and I saw a silver plane storm out of Serbia. The plane thundered over my head, and chasing it I saw a missile, quickly losing height. Hissing, the missile stabbed the river, the rusty cross, the drowned church underneath. A large, muddy finger shook at the sky.

I wrote Vera right away. *When Sister died I thought half of my world ended. With my parents, the other half. I thought these deaths were meant to punish me for something. I was chained to this village, and the pull of the bones below me was impossible to escape. But now I see that these deaths were meant to set me free, to get me moving. Like links in a chain snapping, one after the other.*

If the church can sever its brick roots so can I. I'm free at last,
so wait for me. I'm coming as soon as I save up some cash.

★

Not long after, a Greek company opened a chicken factory in the village. My job was to make sure no bad eggs made it in the cartons. I saved some money, tried to drink less. I even cleaned the house. In the basement, in a dusty chestnut box, I found the leather shoes, the old forgotten flowers. I cut off the toe caps and put them on, and felt so good, so quick and light. Unlucky, wretched brothers. No laces, worn out soles from walking in circles. Where will you take me?

I dug up the two jars of money I kept hidden in the yard and caught a bus to town. It wasn't hard to buy American dollars. Back in the village I lay carnations on the graves and asked the dead for forgiveness. Then I went to the river. I put most of the money and Vladislav's picture in a plastic bag, tucked the bag in my pocket along with some cash for bribes and with my eyes closed swam towards Srbsko.

Cool water, the pull of current, brown old leaves whirlpooling in clumps. A thick branch flows by, bark gone, smooth and rotten. What binds a man to land or water?

When I stepped on the Serbian bank two guards already held me in the aim of their guns.

'Two hundred,' I said and took out the soaking wad.

'We could kill you instead.'

'Or give me a kiss. A pat on the ass?'

They started laughing. The good thing about our countries, the reassuring thing that keeps us falling harder, is that if you can't buy something with money, you can buy it with a lot of money. I counted off two hundred more.

They escorted me up the road, to a frontier post where I paid the last hundred I'd prepared. A Turkish TIR driver agreed to take me to Beograd. There I caught a cab and showed an envelope Vera had sent me.

'I need to get there,' I said.

'You Bulgarian?' the cab driver asked.

'Does it matter?'

'Well, shit. If you're Serbian, that's fine. But if you're a Bugar, it isn't. It's also not fine if you are Albanian, or a Croat. And if you are Muslim, well, shit, then it also isn't fine.'

'Just take me to this address.'

The cab driver turned around and fixed me with his blue eyes.

'I'm gonna ask you once,' he said. 'Are you Bulgarian or are you a Serb?'

'I don't know.'

'Well, then,' he said, 'get the fuck out of my cab and think it over. You ugly-nosed Bulgarian bastard. Letting Americans bomb us, handing over your bases. Slavic brothers!'

Then, as I was getting out, he spat on me.

And now, we are back at the beginning. I'm standing outside Vera's apartment, with flowers in one hand and a bar of Milka in the other. I'm rehearsing the question. I think of how I'm going to greet her, of what I'm going to say. Will the little boy like me? Will she? Will she let me help her raise him? Can we get married, have children of our own? Because I'm finally ready.

An iron safety grid protects the door. I ring the bell and little feet run on the other side.

'Who's there?' a thin voice asks.

'It's Nose,' I say.

'Step closer to the spyhole.'

I lean forward.

'No, to the lower one.' I kneel down so the boy can peep through the hole drilled at his height.

'Put your face closer,' he says. He's quiet for a moment. 'Did Mama do that?'

'It's no big deal.'

He unlocks the door, but keeps the iron grid between us.

'Sorry to say it, but it looks like a big deal,' he says in all seriousness.

'Can I come in?'

'I'm alone. But you can sit outside and wait until they return. I'll keep you company.'

We sit on both sides of the grid. He is a tiny boy and looks like Vera. Her eyes, her chin, her bright, white face. All that will change with time.

'I haven't had Milka in forever,' he says when I pass him the chocolate through the grid. 'Thanks, Uncle.'

'Don't eat things a stranger gives you.'

'You are no stranger. You're Nose.'

He tells me about kindergarten. About a boy who beats him up. His face is grave. Oh, little friend, those troubles now seem big.

'But I'm a soldier,' he says, 'like Daddy. I won't give up. I'll fight.'

Then he is quiet. He munches on the chocolate, offers me a block that I refuse.

'You miss your dad?' I say. He nods.

'But now we have Dadan and Mama is happy.'

'Who's Dadan?' My throat gets dry.

'Dadan,' the boy says. 'My second father.'

'Your second father,' I say and rest my head against the cold iron.

'He's very nice,' the boy says. 'Yes, very nice.'

He talks, sweet voice, and I struggle to resist the venom of my thoughts.

The elevator arrives with a rattle. Its door slides open, bright light out of the cell. Dadan, tall, handsome in his face, walks out with a string bag of groceries – potatoes, yoghurt, green onions, white bread. He looks at me and nods confused.

Then out comes Vera. Bright, speckled face, firm sappy lips.

'My God,' she says. The old spot grows red above her lip and she hangs on my neck.

I lose my grip, the earth below my feet. It feels then like everything is over. She's found someone else to care for her, she's built a new life in which there is no room for me. In a moment,

I'll smile politely and follow them inside, eat the dinner they feed me – musaka with tarator. I'll listen to Vladislav sing songs and recite poems. Then, while Vera tucks him in, I'll talk to Dadan, or rather he'll talk to me, about how much he loves her, about *their* plans, and I will listen and agree. At last he'll go to bed, and under the dim kitchen light Vera and I will wade deep into the night. She'll finish the wine Dadan shared with her for dinner, she'll put her hand on mine. 'My dear Nose,' she'll say, or something to that effect. But even then I won't find courage to speak. Broken, not having slept all night, I'll rise up early, and cowardly again, I'll slip out and hitchhike home.

'My dear Nose,' Vera says now and really leads me inside the apartment, 'you look beaten from the road.' Beaten, is the word she uses. And then, it hits me, the way a hoe hits a snake over the skull. This is the last link of the chain falling. Vera and Dadan will set me free. With them, the last connection to the past is gone.

Who binds a man to land or water, I wonder, if not that man himself?

'I've never felt so good before,' I say, and mean it, and watch her lead the way through the dark hallway. I am no river, but I'm not made of clay.

Sanctuary

Henrietta Rose-Innes

I USED TO drive that long road with my parents, when they were alive. We had a special place we went to camp, and after their death I tried to go back every year or two. It never felt dangerous to be alone at that secret campsite, because of its isolation – who'd know I was there? Of course the trip had its worries. If the car broke down, it might be a long time before anyone passed by.

On that road, the fences are the only thing standing proud of the earth. I mean the old wire sheep-fences, held up by wooden posts and anchored by stones dragged from the fields. They have some power, these fences: in the old days, they put a stop to the springbok migrations. Those great herds don't exist anymore. It's all sheep now, and not too many of them on this dry soil. Still, the livestock is worth enough to keep penned in, and so: hundreds of kilometres of wire, pegging out the land into squares, rhombuses, huge dusty parallelograms, the greater geometry only discernible to some godlike being above in the hot blue sky.

The gravel road penetrates by means of gates; each fence-crossing must be stopped for, negotiated. Some are marked with rough hand-lettered signs – *maak hek toe* – but generally the importance of closing these gates is understood. Each one is a test. Each farmer has his way, his own cobbled-together trademark technique for keeping the gate latched. A mechanism too clever for sheep, not too clever for the rare tourist. Some are pins and some are chains, some hooks and some shackles. Some are sturdily home-engineered from sections of pipe; some just twists of rusty wire. Once you've passed through five or six of these variants, you grow more fluent in the language of latch and hasp; but still, it is a tedious business, the opening and the closing. It's better to have someone along with you, on gate duty. When I used to travel with my parents, I was always the one to nip out, bare feet hurting on the hot stones, and wrestle with the bolts.

On this particular, solitary trip, I was feeling more anxious than usual, perhaps because the car had been acting up. After passing through each gate, I felt momentary paranoia, the urge to go back and check that I'd closed it properly. I imagined sheep streaming through the swinging gate; consequences. But the further I went the harder it seemed to turn around. The thought of latching and unlatching all those farm gates in reverse was exhausting. And so I continued, locking myself deeper and deeper into the countryside.

I was actually glad to see another vehicle: at first just a cloud of orange dust, but which clarified to show the boxy shape of a large new four-by-four, stopped at the gate ahead of me. A woman hopped out of the passenger seat to deal with the gate. I was annoyed that she closed it behind them: it meant a double trip for me, to fiddle with the thing both before and after driving through. But by the next gate, the woman had noticed me, and after that she left the gate open for me at each stop. She was a big woman, but moving quickly, as if harried. Each time, she turned her head to stare at me – seemed almost to be seeking out my eyes – and then turned quickly back, as if someone had snapped at her from inside the car. She hurried to drag the long metal gate through its arc in the dust. The driver waited for her quite far down the road, further than was necessary. She had to trot to catch up, and the car started rolling forward almost before she had the door closed. I couldn't see much through the dust-caked rear window, but I could tell: a bully was in the driver's seat.

At the sixth or seventh gate, things had escalated. The woman was left behind, clutching the top bar of the gate as the vehicle roared away, covering her in dust. I drove up cautiously, pausing to assess the scene. Their car did not stop, did not turn around for her.

She closed the gate behind me and came up to the passenger door. When I let her in, she did not bother with a smile.

'Thank you.'

'Are you all right?' I asked.

She nodded tightly. She wore a khaki blouse and slacks. Her large cheeks would be sheened with sweat if she hadn't been powdered matte with pale orange dust.

'He's just in a mood,' she said. 'He'll be up ahead.' She pressed her curly, sweat-darkened hair back with her palms, leaving streaks on her temples. She had rather large, staring eyes: I could see only the right-hand one, from the side, as she kept her stare fixed on the road ahead. 'He's got the boys with him,' she said after a pause.

Five minutes later, we came upon the next gate. The four-by-four was crouched there, waiting. We pulled up behind. The woman let herself out with a polite thank-you and went to open the gate for him as before. On the other side, she climbed back into their car as if nothing had happened. Now I could see the tops of small heads in the back seat: the boys. The air inside my car crackled with the tension and unhappiness of the departed woman. She'd left a patch of dust on the passenger seat, a handprint clamped onto the door handle.

There were no more gates: the four-by-four

took a turn to the left, onto the tarred driveway of a new nature reserve. It was a fancy place, the first on this road with a high game fence. The entrance was an archway constructed of two fake elephant tusks curving into the sky, although there were no longer any elephants in this part of the world. Khaya Leone Lion Sanctuary, said the concrete sign, faux-carved into faux-ivory.

I carried on along the gravel road, now fenced on one side by the gleaming grid of the two-metre game fence. After a few kilometres the fence turned a corner and marched away into the landscape, dead straight, leaving me alone again with the gravel road.

My turnoff, a narrow track not wide enough for two cars abreast, was easier to spot than I'd feared. As soon as I'd taken it I relaxed and felt better: less observed, more securely alone. I'd made good time and it was still afternoon. I found the old campsite without trouble, and it was the same as ever: the still, cool air under the thorn trees, the white sand, the ruin of an old mud-wall homestead with owls and doves in its eaves and the bones of a sheep, bleached white, inside next to the fireplace. Nothing changed here except for the incremental operations of nature at its quietest: the slow expansion of a wasp nest, a fallen tree surrendering to humus. New-hatched spiders spinning old patterns. And above all, the river. Such a surprise: the moistening and cooling as you picked your way down the bank; the luxurious sweep of shining slate-coloured water glimpsed through the branches.

Here the water was quite deep and smooth. Upstream, to the left, the river cut into the land that had seemed so flat, opening up a rocky passage, with little rapids, a modest ravine, a series of miniature cliffs.

I took my shoes off and felt the mud on my feet, and walked deeper, pursuing the pleasure of the cool water as it inched up my calves. I hadn't realised how parched I'd been. I stripped down to my bra and panties and paddled out, losing the river bottom at times. The current was very slow, barely noticeable, and it was easy to wade upstream, swimming through the deeper spots, occasionally cutting my feet where the water rushed white over the stony bed. I sang to myself: old campfire songs.

But on the opposite bank, something new. A game fence came down to the water to drink, taut and shining, two metres high. A board attached to it said *Khaya Leone, Trespassers will be Prosecuted*. And shortly after that, just around the bend, stood a big house built of raw-looking red wood, low-slung and modern, with a deck stretching out over the water. There was no sign of life – the curtains were drawn – but I doggy-paddled quickly past, putting the house behind me and out of sight. I crossed over some rocks where the water grew shallow, and waded upstream until I felt the solitude seal around me again. Still, something was spoilt.

I rested on a rock for a while like a crocodile,

and then, as the sun moved down the sky, began to drift downstream. Three blond children stood in the shallows, their bright heads bent over the streaming stones. They were laughing and tossing small stones into the deeper pools, skipping them with practised gestures. The oldest boy made one zing out of his snapped fingers with a noise like a bumblebee. I looked around for the parents, because these three boys were very young to be here by themselves – the oldest nine or ten, the others younger still. When they saw me they stopped smiling and stood straight, in a row. Made shy by their identical stares, I tried to keep my underwear submerged, scampering awkwardly over the exposed stones and plunging back into the waist-deep water. I smiled at them gamely and the smallest – not more than five years old – raised a hand.

Still, it was nice to see children so free, I thought: barefoot boys, their soles tough enough not to flinch on the pebbles. City children would be shoed and daubed in sunscreen and never allowed out by themselves in the first place.

As I floated around the next bend I noticed a familiar vehicle in the car-port of the wooden house. The big curly-haired woman was sitting on the dock, her pants rolled to the knee and her feet in the stream. Like her sons she gave me an unsmiling look, a hesitant wave. A man – her husband, must be – was sitting further back in the shade of the patio, a beer on the ground next to his camp chair. I was surprised to see the rifle laid across his knees, but then I realised: Khaya Leone was probably one of those places people came to hunt. Canned lions, maybe. I floated on past, feeling less inclined to like the family.

As I pulled myself out of the water and walked back to my camp, my feet prickling in the thorny ground, I was angry. These people so close, and the game park spread to both sides of the river... they must have built a bridge, further upstream. My boundless isolation was gone. Maybe I should just leave again, despite the long way I'd driven. Not tonight, but first thing tomorrow.

After the sun set I went up the low koppie behind the ruined house and looked down on the opposite shore: the house was right there, very close, paraffin lamps lit on the patio. The man was poking coals in the braai and drinking another beer, but the woman and children were out of sight. He was a rangy, tanned man, his face darkened by stubble. When he lifted his head, alert and listening, I felt myself go rigid like a wild creature in hiding. He called into the house, and I backed down the hillside before the woman could come out. I was sure her curious, beseeching gaze would find me out.

That night I laid out my sleeping bag in the sand as we always used to do, but things were different, wrong: tiny insects feasted on my face and my feet, and the sleeping bag was too hot to zip closed. All night I heard new things; not just the ticking of the cooling earth, not just the night calls of the frogs, but ambiguous, threatening sounds. They might just have been the conversation of water and frogs, but in my half-dreaming, itching state they could also be footsteps, scheming human speech, and at one point something that sounded like roaring. I must have drowsed off, because some sharp rupture jerked me awake in the early-morning hours, and for a panicked moment I knew something big and malevolent was thrashing up through the river reeds. Lions can't swim, I told myself, and fell back into an uneasy sleep.

In the early morning, the boys were standing there at the edge of my campsite, three in a row, barefoot, wearing only underpants. I thought perhaps it was some kind of game they were playing, repaying my visit to their side of the river. But then I saw the tight jaw of the oldest child, and that the two youngest were clutching each others' hands. They must have waded across at the shallow part of the river. It would not have been so shallow for the littlest boy, who looked soaked from head to toe, his hair slicked back against his small skull. They were wiry kids, narrow-hipped, long-legged and knob-kneed, not frail but with no flesh to spare. Their little-boy underpants, damp, clung to their groins. I noticed a blue bruise on the oldest boy's ribcage. More than anything they looked cold. I wanted to cover them in blankets, wrap them in towels.

'What's happened?' I asked.

The oldest boy had clamped his mouth so tight I imagined I could hear his milky teeth grinding in his mouth. The smallest boy started crying. The middle child opened his mouth and the freed voice came out in a shout: 'It was a *lion!*' Then he started to cry too, and the youngest gave a whoop of caught breath and began to howl even harder.

The older boy came forward, as if to speak to me confidentially, but he had no control of his voice either and it came out loud: 'Our ma said we must come across. Pa's got hurt.'

'By a *lion!*'

The fright came through me in a cold ripple. 'Get in the car,' I said.

They obeyed me quickly, with what seemed like relief. I opened the car and then locked them in, all three in the back seat. These children seemed accustomed to silent compliance.

'Stay here, ok? Sit tight.'

The oldest nodded, voice gone again.

Out of the boot I fetched a water bottle, a chocolate bar and some oranges, the few spare t-shirts and towels I had. I opened the car and passed the stuff back to the boys, then cracked the window down a bit - thinking of overheated dogs in cars — and closed the door and locked it. On second thoughts I tossed the keys through to the back seat.

'Keep inside, ok? Keep it locked.'

Nods.

'Your father, does he need an ambulance? Is your mom ok? Your ma?'

The boys looked frightened. The littlest bit down on an orange.

I went back to the river and it seemed deeper, much too deep for such young kids to have attempted it. The water was still dark in the morning shade, and felt silky and thick against my skin as I went in: harder to push aside, the current more insistent. When I came around the bend I swam across the width of the stream and pulled myself up onto the wooden deck of the house, and crouched there for a moment, listening. No sound except a small bird piping, somewhere off in the bush.

Inside, it was too neat for a holiday house. I looked into each room in turn, seeing folded towels, stacked plates. Nothing was disturbed, nothing out of place. I felt strange and wild here, tracking river mud across the swept wooden floors. I went through the back door into the vehicle bay, checking the empty seats of the four-by-four. The light was brighter out back.

Behind the car-port was a row of casuarinas, shedding their messy needles, and beyond that I found myself in a dry field, cultivated once but now given over to small tough succulents, sharp red-brown pebbles and patches of shattered stone pavement. I was barefoot but I barely felt the thorns. The field was empty, but halfway across it was a pile of large stones, probably hauled there when the farmer first cleared the field. Beyond the field I could see the grid of the game fence, its top edge glinting in the new sun. I sniffed the air. How bright the tiny flowers, white and yellow; but there was a tang of something else, something sharp and dirty, running like a wire through the perfect blue air.

Something was wrong with that pile of stones. Something stuck out from behind it at ground level: a grey, blunt point. The stones were piled maybe a metre high. High enough to hide any scene I might imagine, however gruesome. High enough to hide the long crouched body of a lioness. With each step I took forward, the greyish nub became clearer, more comprehensible: it turned into the toe of a shoe. A running shoe. I could see a white sock. A hairy ankle.

I stood quite still for long time, trembling lightly, watching that foot in its shoe. It did not move. I tried to feel on my skin if there was a slight breeze, and which way it was carrying my scent. I altered the angle of my approach: I came silently over the stones, first climbing and then creeping, pressing my belly to the hot warming curve of the topmost rock. Moving forward in millimetres, I peered over, and down.

Very close to mine was a man's forehead. He was sitting against the rocks, and his lined, red-burnt face was turned up to mine, the jaw slack to show the grey teeth of his lower jaw. In the centre of his forehead was a clean red hole. A red line ran down from it into his eye. The lion's tooth, I thought. I looked into his drying blue eye. There was no lion there.

The backs of my knees started to prickle

from the sun, and a small black lizard crept out and over the back of my hand and vanished into a crack in the reddish stone. Quietly, so as not to disturb the lizard or any other creature, I lowered myself down from the pile of rocks and stepped carefully back though the grass towards the house. I walked along the row of trees but there was no sign of the woman in their meagre shade. Perhaps I should call out for the wife, make some kind of noise, but I knew there would be no sound coming from my chest. My jaws were clamped tight shut. Then I remembered about the children.

The swim back across the river was hard, wearying; my muscles were tired. Perhaps I had just gone back and forth too many times. I felt like one more crossing would sink me.

I didn't have much to pack up: I had barely made camp the night before, just unrolling my sleeping bag on the sand. The interior of my car was hot and filled with the mucousy odour of children's distress. The younger children were asleep or pretending to be, but the oldest was wide awake, his bony knees sticking out from under my too-large t-shirt. I held out my hand for the car keys.

'Did you see it?' he asked.

I didn't know what to say. I shook my head.

'The lion? Did you see it?'

'No, no I didn't see the lion.'

I couldn't drive at first, with the trembling in my hands, so I busied myself by checking that the boys were wrapped in t-shirts and towels, although that was hardly what they needed in the growing heat; that they drank water and passed around the tube of gumdrops from the glove compartment. At last I backed the car away from the quiet clearing, saying goodbye to the resident owl. Disturbed, it drifted silently from the crumbling window of the mud house, through the morning air and into the trees. As we drove away, our wheels covered the place in dust.

She was standing at the entrance to the game lodge, the absurd tusks casting bars of morning shadow over her face. She held the long gun carelessly in one hand, dragging the butt in the gravel as she came forward to meet us.

'Let's leave that behind, shall we,' I said.

She shrugged, and laid the rifle down on the road next to her.

'They might need it,' she said.

'Who?'

'The police.'

I thought about this. 'Okay. Then put it in the boot. It's open.'

Obedient, she picked the gun up again and went round to the back of the car and laid the gun sideways in the boot, then came back and took her place on the passenger seat.

'Hello Ma,' said the oldest boy, and she looked at him levelly in the rear-view mirror. 'Hello my boy,' she said.

And so we headed back, along the same route

as before, with the quiet boys in the back. At one point the eldest stirred and pushed his hand through the gap between the seats to touch his mother's arm. She jumped a little and I realised how much tension was in her slow form. Her arms were folded across her bosom and with just the fingertips of her left hand she trapped the son's fingertips against the flesh of her bicep and held it there.

She was docile. At each farm gate we stopped and she left the car and opened the latch and pulled the long arm of the gate through its arc in the dust. I drove through and waited while she did up the complex metal knot, and then we moved on again, making good our slow, methodical escape. Over and over again we did this, locking ourselves out for good, locking it all away behind us: the owls and the lions, the tiny flowers and the wasps. The sand and the red rocks. The deep, cool river.

In the Basement

Adam Ross

WE WERE AT Nicholas and Maria's house, watching the video of their ultrasound. They'd decided they didn't want to know the sex of the baby before it was born, so the technician had edited the tape for them. But Maria was finishing her residency in internal medicine, so perhaps there were clues in the image only she could see, something about the shape of the foetus's winking heart that indicated a girl, or a rhythm to the dusty blood flow that revealed a boy. If she guessed, she didn't let on. She serenely watched it, as if conducting a conversation with her child, cataloguing all the secrets and stories she would tell, the bedside songs she would sing, the mistakes she might prevent. We sat in their living room. It was winter in Nashville and we'd had a week of snow. It was snowing even now. In the mornings I woke to a world of uniform greyness, the trees on the powdered hills bristly and charred, the sky as colourless as the screen in front of us.

137

I found the ultrasound disturbing. I'd never seen one before and the unborn child seemed to me a mutant creature, barely human. The figure was so striated that it was like looking at the fossil of an embryo, as if the foetus was carved out of bone. It lay at the base of a cone of light, feet up, hands curled near its mouth. When it moved you could see ribs fanning along the axis of its spine, reminding me of the sinuous skeletons of snakes. As the technician moved the probe over Maria's belly, orbiting the child, the image took on a funhouse-mirror quality, the baby's face suddenly elongated like a Munch painting, its eyes two enormous dotted sockets, its head distinguishable as two separate interlocking parts: jaw attached to skull, skull arching over the eyes like a centurion's helmet.

'That's the brain plate,' Maria explained. The foetus seemed to stare out at us from the television, then twitched convulsively and came to rest again.

Nicholas said he thought it was a boy. He sat on the couch next to my wife, Carla. He hadn't taken his eyes off the screen, and when he said this he stuck out his hand and gestured, laughing. 'It *is*,' he insisted, as if it were self-evident, as if proclaiming it made it so. 'Look at it,' he said. 'Look at *him*.' And suddenly I saw a clear resemblance to Nicholas in the protruding brow, the discretely prominent chin, the distance from the mouth to the eyes suggesting the same small nose that Nicholas had.

And I thought, Of course it's a boy. Of course
Nicholas would exercise his will even over Maria's
womb. And of course Maria would have a son
when she needed a daughter – an ally against
Nicholas and this life in which he surrounded and
enclosed her.

'Let's turn this off,' he said after a while.

'All right,' Maria said, picking up the remote
to pause the tape. The image of the creature-child
hung there, frozen.

We were at that point after dinner when it
isn't clear what to do next. Carla got up to get
more wine. Maria cleared some plates and followed
her to the kitchen, even though Carla had told her
to stay put. Nicholas and I had to get up from our
seats in order to let them out of the room. He and
Maria had long ago outgrown this dank little place,
a nondescript brick duplex, but Nicholas hadn't
had a job in almost two years. He was eight years
into his philosophy doctorate, struggling to
complete a dissertation on the pre-Socratics that
he'd never been able to explain to me. They
couldn't afford to move on Maria's salary alone. To
compensate, Nicholas had made all sorts of home
improvements. In the living room he'd installed a
bike rack hung from the ceiling. For all their
books, he'd run track shelving on the adjacent wall.
In the kitchen he'd erected a wooden countertop
over their washer and dryer, a contraption that
folded open on hinges, the machines half visible
beneath it like a pair of caged animals. Above their

bed he'd wired a pair of reading lights into the walls and built floating shelves into the corners so they could squeeze in the largest mattress possible. Most ingenious was the changing station he'd fashioned in the closet of the nursery, a table that slid out like a keyboard plate with storage for diapers and blankets in the drawers below. Their place reminded me of a nuclear bunker – a testament to Nicholas's insistence on using every inch of space they had. (He'd worked construction to pay for college tuition but now – with a child on the way and an unborn dissertation – he wasn't doing anything). Despite all this, there was no room in the apartment for a Christmas tree, so they'd hung a wreath over Maria's small piano and stood all their cards below it.

One of them caught my eye, and Nicholas noticed me staring.

'She's drop-dead, isn't she?'

It was a photograph of a husband and wife and their two young children, a boy and a girl, the family on a beach somewhere luxurious, though nothing captured your attention like the woman. She was incredibly beautiful.

Nicholas smiled. 'Ever seen two uglier kids?'

Their homeliness was as remarkable as their mother's beauty. I looked at the card again. It was a pleasure to be able to stare at the woman so unabashedly. She had long, curly brown hair, blue eyes so pale they seemed lit from within.

The girls returned. When Maria noticed

which photograph I was looking at she said 'Oh' and tucked her chin into her neck. 'That's Lisa.'

'Tell them the story about Lisa,' Nicholas said.

'You tell them.'

'No, you tell it.'

Maria sat down gingerly, adjusting her skirt. Then she looked at her chest and brushed herself off, as if she were covered in crumbs. 'I don't know where to start,' she said.

'Start at the beginning. At school.'

Maria reached over to the table, picked up her wineglass, took a sip, and put it down. Marx and Weber, their two German shepherds, squeezed past the coffee table and curled themselves neatly around her feet, having grown noticeably more protective during her pregnancy. She bent forward to pet them, then leaned back in her chair.

'Lisa,' she said, 'was my best friend in college. We became close when we were sophomores in chemistry, and we shared an apartment together our senior year, the year that Nicholas and I met. She was gorgeous, just like you see her now, but I don't know, she seemed even more so then. Do you agree with that?'

Nicholas shrugged. He ran his palm across his short black hair. When we met them two years ago, he wore it long, down to his shoulders, but now he cut it himself. He was half Russian and a quarter Cherokee, with Asian eyes and the full lips of a Mongol. He'd played football in college, and his body still had some of that absurd mass.

'Go on,' he said.

'She was also brilliant. No, that's not even right. She was one of the most intelligent and creative people I've ever met. She was a big star in the English department and a dual major in biology. She could paint, too, and didn't she come to school on a dance scholarship?'

Nicholas nodded.

Maria took another sip of wine. 'Anyway, when you were around her you couldn't help but think how nice it must be to have unlimited options in life. And yet you couldn't hate her or be jealous – at least I couldn't – because she was so kind. She was good. She was *good,* wasn't she?' she said to the dogs. They lifted their heads, waited, then put them down and sighed. 'She had nothing to be afraid of,' Maria said. 'I remember that fall we were all talking about what we were going to do with ourselves next, and Lisa had all sorts of glamorous plans – teach English in Japan, work for Doctors Without Borders, go to Africa for the UN. And I supported anything she suggested without question because somehow I needed her to do something spectacular.' She looked at Carla. 'Does that make sense?'

Carla had lit a cigarette. She'd opened the window by her to spare us the smoke. 'Absolutely it makes sense,' she said.

Maria paused for a moment. We're close friends, so the silence was comfortable. I poured myself more wine and looked around the room, at all of Nicholas's books, at the bicycle rack and the reading stand he'd made with rollers on its legs and an adjustable desktop so that Maria could work while sitting in their club chair. To make ends meet, she'd been moonlighting regularly at Veterans Hospital, Baptist, and Vanderbilt, seven months pregnant and still picking up killer shifts, twenty-four and sometimes even thirty-six hours on call. And you could look at these things Nicholas had built, these enhancements, as his way of either assisting her or goading her – I wasn't sure which. According to mutual friends, three years ago, before we knew them, Nicholas had an affair with one of his graduate students, and he and Maria separated for a time. One afternoon, after he ran out of fellowship money, he snuck over to her apartment, stole a credit card application from the mail, and applied for it under her name. He used this card to fund his life for the next several months, running Maria into enormous debt. And still, after all this, they reconciled. This was a mystery to me. Why had she forgiven him? Why had he come back? Could people really forget or get over such things? Had he crippled her self-esteem? Or were they willing to go to these lengths simply because they loved each other? 'They're either the cursed or the blessed,' Carla once said to me, 'but I'd have kicked that son of a bitch out long ago' – which at the time I took as a warning. On the other hand, I wasn't sure it was so cut and dried. There's a photograph of the two of them in their living room that I always like to look at whenever I'm over. Nicholas and Maria have their backs to the camera, walking hand in hand along the ridge of some valley in Germany – nothing but mountains beyond and below them for miles. It's fall, so they're wearing sweaters and stocking hats, and because they're on a slope and Nicholas is standing downhill from his wife, they seem the same height, two happy little people, married since forever. And every time I consider this photo, what's clear to me is that it's easier to understand what makes two people let go than what keeps them together.

'Where was I?' Maria said.

'Unlimited options,' said Carla.

'Anyway, by the end of that fall I'd already applied to medical schools, and Nicholas was applying to programmes in philosophy. But Lisa, I don't know how to describe it. She just shut down. It wasn't exactly a nervous breakdown, but something close. She just withdrew – from me, from school, from everything. All her energy left her. Her enthusiasm. Maybe the weight of her options started to overwhelm her or–'

'Oh, come on,' Nicholas said.

'What?'

'You're telling it completely wrong.'

Maria hunched slightly, and her eyes went blank.

'Weight of her options?' he said.

Maria wouldn't look at him. 'Story police,' she said.

'Don't make her such a victim.'

Carla and I had never witnessed them quarrel openly, but we'd seen portents, harbingers of fights waiting to happen the minute we left. '*You* tell it,' she said, sitting back in her chair. Maria stared into space while Nicholas smiled at the two of us. His teeth were spaced widely apart. I tried to catch Carla's eye but she took a long drag on her cigarette and wouldn't look at me.

'First of all,' Nicholas said, 'you have to understand that Lisa wasn't some picture-perfect genius. She was a bit of a head case. You'd agree with *that,* wouldn't you?'

Maria didn't appear to be listening.

Nicholas shook his head. 'Lisa could be *way* out there,' he said. 'She had this need for extravagance, so everything she did had to be extraordinary. And if it wasn't she abandoned it – no matter what it was, or who. That fall she was talking about writing a novel, and she even started one at the beginning of the semester. She signed up for a Creative Writing class and when she came back after the first session she was so excited she could barely contain herself. She was going to write a novel like no one had ever written before, she told me. She thought it was amazing that a narrative form several hundred years old was still chained to linearity and psychological realism – the same Joycean rant all the smart kids make before they bother to write a word. Then she went to her room, closed the door, and set to work – just like that. I'm pretty sure she was up most of the night. Being manic like that, she'd have made a great surgeon. I was basically living with Maria by that time, so when Lisa left for class the next morning, I went in to have a look at what she'd done because I was dying of curiosity.'

'Jealousy,' Maria said.

'Please. The pages were on her desk – fifteen, maybe twenty, drafted in one sitting. She wrote this very mannered prose, but it had a kind of energy that immediately hooked you. But it wasn't really a story per se. It began with this long description of an old doorman in the service elevator of an apartment building. He's collecting tenants' trash and going through it, spinning tales in his mind about what he finds while remembering things he's overheard during his rides with these same people. He's got a portable radio with him in the elevator that's tuned to a call-in show, and the narrative shifts from these on-the-air conversations into what's going on in the guest's head. He's a doctor who's explaining the process of separating conjoined twins, giving all this technical material in layspeak, but then it goes into his memories of the actual operation, passages that only someone with Lisa's knowledge could pull off. That's as far as she got, but it was fantastic stuff. It really was. And I wanted to tell her this. But when I stopped by that evening, she was sitting at her desk holding her hair in one fist and striking through line after line with a black marker. She was crossing everything out in utter disgust. So I knocked lightly on her door, and she glared at me wild-eyed and said, 'I'm *working*,' then reached out and slammed it in my face. She dropped the class a week later.'

Maria stood up; both dogs, suddenly agitated, rose too. 'I need some water,' she said, and went to the kitchen. Carla was looking at Nicholas, slightly amazed, as if she'd never seen him before. She was still ignoring me, and I felt a tightness in my gut, something close to fear. Occasionally, a night with Nicholas and Maria could touch off tensions between the two of us. Carla was twenty-eight and had been practicing law for two years. I was thirty-three, teaching the LSAT, bartending, still struggling to wrap up a novel I'd been working on for a long time. When she got frustrated with me, when we really got into it, she'd say I'd been finishing the book ever since we met – an ungenerous, simplistic accusation, I thought, if not entirely inaccurate. What was inarguably true was that there was a growing list of things we couldn't talk about – the hours I'd put in writing that day, if I'd gone for a run, if Nicholas and I went out for coffee. 'It must be nice,' Carla might say, 'to meet for a leisurely chat in the middle of the afternoon.' I didn't dare answer. I started editing out all sorts of daily information, minimising conversations with my family, growing wary of phone calls that tied up our line. 'Who were you talking to for so long?' Carla might ask when she got through. *Bitch* was often on the tip of my tongue, and I would've said it many times if her questions weren't apt, her frustrations and fears not justified. Worse, these elisions were changing me: I was a miser with good news, with friends' pregnancies, promotions, new homes. When Carla called me out regarding this pettiness, we sometimes spiraled into vicious argument. In the past few months, we'd said unforgettable things.

Maria came back. 'You didn't have to wait,' she said.

Nicholas watched her sit, but she wasn't backing down and I thought they might have it out right then. He wanted some acknowledgment from her, even at our expense. He was so unyielding that in a strange way I admired him. He made *no* apologies. He just took. Yet he never talked to me about Maria, as if their relationship was sacrosanct. Once, over drinks, I'd told him about the problems Carla and I were having; bitter, I offered more details than were necessary, all of which he considered thoughtfully. But finally he replied, 'Never underestimate a woman's loyalty.' I felt so ashamed that I promised myself I'd never discuss my marriage with him again.

'But Maria's right,' he said, relenting. 'Lisa did shut down for a while, but not because she had unlimited options. She just had no follow-through. Everyone around her was making choices on the fly. Plenty of us had no idea what we were getting into, but Lisa didn't understand commitment. She couldn't accept that making a choice eliminates other choices. She wanted to step up and hit the bull's-eye on the first try. She was so talented, so quick, she had no clue how long it really took to get somewhere.'

At this, Maria and Carla simply looked at each other.

'So she overcompensated. We come back from Christmas vacation after Lisa's had her little meltdown, and she's all better. She seems completely restored. We're having dinner together that first night, and out of the blue she announces she's getting married.

'And we're floored. We were like, "Married? To who? *When?*" And she says she just wants to *get* married, she *has* to get married. We think she's joking. But Lisa's like, "I've never been so sure of anything in my life. It's what I want. It's what my mother did, and she's happy. I don't want to be one of those women who have to compete in the rat race. I don't want to work insane hours. I want children. I want to be a *homemaker.* Is that such a dishonourable goal?" And then she lists all the qualities she'd come up with for her ideal mate. She really had a list. He had to be financially secure enough to support her comfortably. She wanted him to be handsome, absolutely. She felt strongly that he should have a solid religious background – Catholic, Jewish, it didn't matter, as long as he believed and practised *something.* It got a lot more specific than that. She'd really put her mind to it. It was all so hyperconscious that I honestly thought she'd gone nuts. And when Maria and I told her she was being obsessive, that this was a misguided grasp at certainty, at a direction, she shot us down. She said we were being hypocritical because we were married already, even though it wasn't official, which was true.

'She went out almost every night that spring, hunting for a husband. It became her job. Her new major. It was the sole purpose of everything she did. She trekked into Seattle and hit the town. She joined a gym off campus. She started going to openings at galleries, to restaurant openings. She asked about the family backgrounds of classmates. She became a database of who was who and who had what. She dragged Maria and me out with her occasionally. And the nights we came along, it was fascinating to watch her size men up, approach them, talk to them or wait until they approached her. And within an hour or sometimes just minutes she'd come back to where we were sitting and compare the guys against her criteria and describe how they'd passed or failed. And the whole time she seemed completely happy.

'But none of them made the cut. I don't think she even slept with anybody. One guy, Thomas, was part of the Heinz or Hellmann's family – directly related to some condiment. Anyway, he took her out regularly and spent many late nights at the apartment, but always left scratching his head. I mean literally. He looked so puzzled that Maria and I started calling him

Doubting Thomas during those last few weeks he held on. And suddenly we stopped seeing him altogether.

'By then we were graduating. Maria and I both got into schools in Oregon and Lisa took a job with a think tank in Washington, DC.'

'No husband?' Carla asked.

'Not even a boyfriend,' Nicholas said.

'Can I see the card?' Carla whispered to Maria, even though I was holding it. Her indirectness made me mildly furious, but I passed it to Maria, who handed it to her, both of us keen to see her reaction to the image – which was one of total indifference.

'Over the next few years,' Nicholas said, 'we began to drift apart. We were busy. She and Maria didn't speak often. She'd gotten into medical school but dropped out after a year and a half. She took a high-paying job in pharmaceutical sales, then quit. She moved to San Francisco and worked for a dot-com startup and was travelling coast to coast all the time. When she and Maria did manage to talk, Lisa mostly discussed the men in her life. If she was still on her quest, she'd made a real mess of it. She'd had an affair with the married CEO of her company, who was going to leave his wife, then he wasn't, at which point Lisa fell into the arms of some journalist she was involved with back in New York. And I thought she'd arrived at the perfect solution to her own character, because I couldn't imagine her tolerating anyone long enough to get to the point of marriage.

'But maybe a year later she calls to tell us that she's in love. His name's Uzi Levi, an Israeli investment banker. They'd been together for two months, and she goes on and on about how successful and handsome he is, that he's everything she could ever hope for, et cetera. She described this whirlwind romance, how on their first date they flew down to Los Angeles for the evening, had dinner in Santa Monica, then drove to a house he'd rented in Malibu. How when she woke up the next morning the view from the bedroom was of nothing but the Pacific, the dolphins swimming, the whales breaching, all typical Lisa-extravagance. And when we asked her what he was *like* she said, "All questions will be answered at our wedding." Again just like Lisa to make such an announcement.

'Have you ever been to a wedding that feels like a horrible mistake? Where every accident seems like an omen? The reception's held outside, and it pours. The bride's father's toast is uncomfortably short. A child wails during the vows. We meet this Uzi Levi and he's thin, balding, charmless – as blunt as a lot of Israelis can be. He had these three girlfriends he'd known since childhood, and they hovered around him the whole time like a bizarre chorus. During the rehearsal dinner, they gave a weird, inappropriate toast, this poem they'd written in couplets full of innuendo about his sexual past with them and his decision to marry outside the fold. And of course it was wrong of us to hold anything against him, because he was the victim of our *own* expectations for Lisa. Everybody's a social Darwinist at a wedding: you want the perfect pairing for a friend. But we just didn't get it. And to see them under the chuppah and watch their two families circle up for the hora – Lisa's WASP contingent and Levi's clan – it was like some bad comedy of intermarriage, the most insane mismatch. I know it sounds like I'm some closet anti-Semite, but that's not it. They were just so completely different it was hard not to think about them in almost animal terms. Meanwhile, the spectacle of it all was off the charts, and God knows how much it cost. When Lisa and I danced she kept me stiffly at arm's length, and when I asked what her plans were she said, "Go on my wonderful honeymoon, take care of my wonderful husband." Everything was so wonderful it was depressing. She smiled, thanked me after the song ended, and then she made her way around the room. Maria and I watched her talk with the other women, putting her hand to their pregnant stomachs and oohing and aahing and showing off her enormous ring – and if this all seems clichéd, it was, and *that's* what stunned us, that she'd transformed herself so utterly. And when she wrote us a thank-you note for our wedding present, she described the private island where they'd honeymooned in excruciating detail: how every couple had an open-air hut and put up a flag when they wanted a meal, how the owner of the resort bred yellow Labs that swam in the surf and ran free in honey-coloured packs. I guessed she'd finally gotten what she wanted.

'After that, we heard from her only when we got the birth announcements. And holiday greetings like that card there – pictures of Lisa and her husband and their kids. Until, a few years later, we get another unexpected phone call.

'She'd latched onto the idea of buying a dog for her children, a German Shepherd, and as soon as she said this I could envision her mind working through a series of associations back to us. We had two Shepherds and would be the ideal resource to consult about this important decision. She made a little small talk but then went right into it: "How are your dogs with kids they meet? Are they too protective with you? Did you cage train?" It was painful talking with her. She'd done some internet research and was full of the concerns that come with superficial knowledge. What about Schutzhund Shepherds? Should she buy from a German breeder? It wasn't surprising that she needed a best-in-show dog with impeccable bloodlines. We got a slew of calls from her over the next few weeks – questions about what to look for in terms of temperament, personality, conformity standards, training techniques – but never any sense that she realised we hadn't spoken in years. Did we use treats or vocal praise? Would a male dog recognise a woman as alpha? Did we let our dogs on the furniture? Were they afraid of blacks? Until finally, after this endless back-and-forth, she called to say she'd bought a puppy, as if we were dying to hear what she'd decided. Naturally, it was a bitch Shepherd she'd had shipped from Germany and paid an arm and a leg for, maybe four thousand dollars, and she was going to train it herself. The children *loved* the dog, and she was *so* enjoying their bonding with it and would send us a picture – and that was it. We didn't hear from her again, though a few weeks later we did get the photo, and of course the puppy was gorgeous, and on the back Lisa had written her name: Eva.

'So a few months later, Maria and I had a wedding to go to in San Francisco. We hadn't seen Lisa since she got married, so we called the week before our trip and made arrangements to stay an extra day afterward to visit with her and meet her kids. We were very curious. I remember how giddy we were as we drove up to Pacific Heights. You always have this preconceived idea of luxury that's rarely fulfilled in reality, but not in this case. It was a white house perched on the highest point in the neighbourhood, with incredible views of the Golden Gate and the bay. It was surrounded by a huge brick wall and had a roof deck like a crow's nest – a widow's walk – with a wrought-iron fence around it. Inside, everything was immaculate and the furniture ultramodern: Viking range, Sub-Zero fridge, shower with jets from five angles, the whole works. After the tour we met the children, who were with the nanny in the third-floor playroom. You could tell the daughter had all of Lisa's intelligence, and the boy was unusually self-possessed, but they were both so *odd*-looking. I don't want this to sound mean but Lisa's perfect features had combined with her husband's in such a twisted way that it made you realise how close beauty can be to its opposite.

'So finally the three of us sit down for coffee. Uzi, Lisa informs us, had been called away on business at the last minute and couldn't join us, which was all we heard about him that afternoon. After we'd been talking for a while, Maria goes, "Wait, where's the *dog*?" And Lisa says, "Oh, we don't let her play in the house." And Maria asks, "Well, is she out back? I didn't see her." And Lisa says, "No. She's downstairs." And Maria's like, "What do you mean?" And Lisa says, "During the day we keep her in the basement." So Maria looks at me, then at Lisa, and finally says, "Well, c'mon, let's go see the girl."

'I'll never forget this until the day I die. Lisa crossed her arms and led us down a narrow wooden staircase to the basement. It was dry and very cool, perfectly clean and bare, as if the house had been vacated or nothing in their lives ever made it to storage. A dim light was shining through the dirty transom windows looking out into the front yard and the flower garden. And in the middle of the room, in the near dark, I could see the kennel – probably the same crate they'd flown her over in.

'A single exposed bulb hung from the ceiling above it, and the moment Lisa flipped the switch I could see the light reflected in the dog's eyes through the bars. It was so small there was barely enough room for her to move. Utterly rigid, she looked at us with her ears pricked up, waiting for Lisa to come to the gate. There was so much love in her eyes, so much patience, as Lisa drew closer, her arms still crossed, and bent down to peer inside. We all stood quietly, and the dog, completely alert, frozen, just waiting, didn't make a sound.

'But *we* waited too. Maria and I were speechless, horrified, waiting like the dog for Lisa to do something, until finally she said, "There she is." She gestured toward the animal with her head. "That's Eva." She waved at her half-heartedly, her other arm still pressed across her chest. "Hello, Eva," she said. This sent a pulse of movement through the cage, which scratched against the floor, jumped slightly. Then Maria looked at Lisa and said, "Let her out. *Now.*"

'The moment Lisa opened the gate you'd have thought the dog was shot from a gun. She ran out and past us up those creaky stairs. Her back legs were asleep, so she lost her footing and tripped as she dragged herself up, her hindquarters splayed out behind her. And then, at the top of the landing, she *waited* for us in the kitchen.

'The dog was completely out of control. She was so submissive that as soon as I got upstairs and made eye contact with her she pissed all over the floor. She was so desperate for company that she mouthed like a pup, jumping and pawing at us all, barking and running wild in tight circles as if she were chasing her tail, and then she squatted to shit. Meanwhile Lisa was leaning against the door, calmly watching the whole scene as Maria and I tried to settle Eva down. Lisa just stood there, slowly shaking her head. "You see? This is why we can't let her in the house. She *pees* everywhere. She jumps. She knocks things over. She S-H-I-Ts on the floor. It's just terrible." And I said to her, "My God, Lisa, how can you treat an animal like this?" The dog had her mouth on my wrist, pulling at me. And Lisa told me, "Honestly, Nicholas, I was very patient with her, but it didn't help a bit."

'Maria and I couldn't stay after that. We looked at each other, and without saying a word we had this silent exchange: Do we take the dog with us? No, we can't. But we will *never* speak with this person again.

'So we left. We made these embarrassed, hurried good-byes, then drove down toward the bay. We didn't say anything for several minutes. I think we were both in shock. And then Maria broke down, sobbing her heart out. You remember how you cried?' Nicholas said.

But she wasn't looking at him, just sitting there, looking at the image on the television screen, swirling her wine.

'Anyway,' Nicholas said, 'we haven't spoken to Lisa since. She still sends us Christmas cards, though I don't think she gives us a thought. I mean, I'm sure it never occurs to her that we're people she no longer knows. We're just another thing on her list of a million things to do.'

It was snowing harder now than before. I could feel the heat escaping through the front door, could see the accumulation rising on the sill and honeycombing the panes, streaming down through the streetlight like so much dust.

'So that's the story,' Nicholas said.

Carla and I cleared the rest of the dishes. We told Maria to stay in her chair and rest, and asked Nicholas not to move, though from the living room he said we should just leave the whole mess by the sink; he'd take care of it in the morning. Maria had leaned her head back against her chair, and within minutes she was asleep. We didn't even consider waking her up to say good-bye.

Carla and I walked home. It was beautiful outside, with no cars on the road and no traffic noise at all, and for a long time we just absorbed this quiet world falling around us. The tension I'd felt between us had dissipated in the cold, which forced us to lock arms as we slipped and slid together. Our laughter at each surprising misstep sounded like the only laughter on earth, and we spoke only of the night and the snow until we got close to home. We stopped to look at our house blanketed in powder, as if to make sure we'd taken its true measure. And then Carla said she loved me, that she wanted me to finish my book, that she knew I could. She wanted us to have a child soon. She hated Nicholas, I *had* to know she did, and she didn't want her life to be like Maria's. I assured her that would never happen. I gave her my word, and to make sure she believed me I enumerated all of Nicholas's failures. I rehashed all the unpleasant things he didn't know we knew about him, like I was going down a checklist of faults I didn't have. I talked for a long time, longer than I should have. I kept talking even after my eyes no longer held hers, Carla staring instead at her feet. And in that moment of weakness, I hoped that she might look on me afterward and feel lucky.

Before He Left the Family

Carrie Tiffany

BEFORE HE LEFT the family, my father worked as a sales representative for a pharmaceutical company. He travelled from chemist to chemist with samples of pills and lotions and pastes in the back of his Valiant station wagon. The best sales representatives visited modern chemists in the city and suburbs. My father had to drive long distances to country chemists who had stocked the same product lines for years and weren't interested in anything new. As he drank more and more, my father called on fewer and fewer chemists, but the cardboard boxes of samples kept arriving. They no longer fitted in the back of the car, so my father stored them in the corrugated iron shed next to the house. Summer in Perth is very hot. For months and months the bitumen boiled on the roads and we had to use the ends of our t-shirts to open the iron lid of the mailbox, or risk getting burnt. The pharmaceutical samples expanded in the heat of the shed. The lotions and pastes burst their tubes and tubs and seeped through the cardboard boxes. It smelt good in the shed – sweet and clean and surgical. My brother and I went in there often and sat among the sodden boxes as we read our father's *Playboy* magazines.

In the last weeks of their marriage, our parents battled out the terms of their separation at the dinner table in between the ice-cream bowls. My mother, small and freckled, wrote lists of their possessions on a Nordette® Low Dose Oral Contraceptive notepad. She looked like a teenage girl playing a board game. Nathan and I listened in as we watched television on the other side of the vinyl concertina doors that marked the division between the lounge room and the dining room. We watched *MASH*. Nathan sang along to the theme song, and for the first time I noticed how high and piping his voice was. And there was something creepy about his pink skin and the cowlick at the front of his fine white hair. I wondered if we hadn't created a masculine enough environment for our father. I tipped my brother out of his chair and started boxing his arms and chest. He wailed. The doors were dragged open.

'Kevin, what are you doing?' my mother said, leaning against the buckled vinyl as if she was too young to stand unsupported. I let Nathan squirm out from underneath me.

'He's a sissy,' I said. 'He sings like a girl. Tell

him he's not allowed to sing.'

She looked from me to Nathan and back to me again; then she forced her eyes open wide so they boggled with exasperation.

The playmates in the *Playboy* magazines are always smiling. Or, if they aren't smiling they have a gasping, pained expression as if they've just stood on a drawing pin. None of them have someone special in their lives at this time, but with the right man they can be hot to handle. They like the feeling of silk against their bare skin, and they appreciate the outdoors and candle-lit dinners. Miss July says she likes the heat (she's from Queensland), but on the next page she says she would like to make love in the snow. This contradiction seems to have slipped past the *Playboy* editor. I wonder if this is a concern to other readers? The skin of the playmates can be matched to the samples of different timber stains that we have in woodwork class. The brunettes are teak or mahogany, the blondes are stained pine if they have a tan, or unstained pine if they are from Sweden, Finland, Denmark, or the Netherlands. The playmates don't have veins showing through their skin – it is just the one colour – like a pelt. And none of them have freckles or bits of hardened sleep in the corner of their eyes like tiny potatoes.

My father agreed to take only his personal items; his clothes, shoes, records, golf clubs, and alcohol.

On the morning that he left I stood in the driveway and waved him off. My mother and brother watched from the kitchen window. My father's work shirts hung in rows down each side of the rear of the station wagon. It looked neat – like it had been designed for that purpose – like a gentleman's wardrobe on wheels. My father waved his forearm out of the window as he drove off. Just as he rounded the bend in the road and the car moved out of sight, he tooted his horn. I stood and watched for a few minutes. When I finally turned to walk away, I noticed my mother and brother were still looking out of the kitchen window; but now they were looking at me.

My father married my mother when she was eighteen, because he had made her pregnant. It was just the one time; the one date. My mother had a job interview at the shoe shop where my father was working. She didn't get the job, but my father, the junior sales clerk, asked her out. When my brother and I were little we often asked our father to tell us the story of how he met our mother. He always said the same thing. He said that our mother had the best pair of knockers he'd ever seen. For many years my brother and I believed that knockers were a brand of shoe. It was through reading the *Playboy* magazines hidden among the boxes of pharmaceutical samples in the shed that I realised my mistake. And although we never spoke of it, I believe that Nathan, who is three years younger than me, was also enlightened this way.

I heard my father's car in the driveway a few days after he left. My mother was at her bootscooting class and Nathan had gone along to watch. The Valiant was empty and I wanted to ask my father where he was living, where all his shirts were hanging now, but it felt too intrusive. My father called me over to help him load the stereo, the fan, a china dinner service that had never been out of its box, an Esky, and a bodybuilding machine into the back of his car. I knew that my mother would be angry, but I felt flattered my father had asked me for help with the lifting. No man ever refused to help another man lift.

A week later, my father came back again and tried to remove some of the boxes of pharmaceutical samples from the shed. My mother rushed out of the house as soon as she saw his car. She shrieked at him and tried to block the doorway to the shed. My father pushed past her. Nathan started to whimper. I stood near the tailgate of the Valiant – I hoped that my father would think I was trying to help him, and that my mother would think I was trying to stop him. My mother saw one of our neighbours working in his garden over the fence and she called out to him. She insisted that he help her, saying that my father was trying to steal her property. Ron looked uncomfortable, but he came and leant against the fence, holding his small soil-stained trowel in his hand.

'G'day, Ron,' my father said, cheerfully, as he carried a stack of cardboard boxes towards the car.

My mother rushed at him then, and they grappled with the boxes. Some of the boxes disintegrated as my mother and father snatched at them. Ron banged his trowel against the fence palings to signal his disapproval. I was embarrassed for all of us. It was unseemly. The pieces of soft cardboard on the ground looked dirty and cheap. The value of us – the whole family enterprise – seemed to be symbolised by them.

My father never came to the house again. He took a job interstate. The telephone calls became less and less frequent, then they stopped. The first year, with the anticipation that he might write or ring on our birthdays or at Christmas, was confusing, but things settled down after that.

Because my father left Western Australia and my mother didn't know where he was working, she was unable to have any maintenance payments taken out of his wages. Money was tight. When the windscreen of the Torana shattered, my mother covered it in gladwrap and kept driving. She took a job with the local real estate agent. She didn't have her licence, so she answered the telephone and wrote down messages. On the weekends the owner of the agency let her put up directional signs in the streets surrounding houses they had listed for sale. He told her it was good experience and would help her when she sat the exam for her estate agent's licence.

One Saturday morning Nathan and I went

along to help our mother with the signs. The signs were metal; they attached to a steel stake with wire. There was a rubber mallet to bang the steel stakes into the ground. The house for sale was on a recent estate behind the tip. A new road had been built to get into the estate so that the residents didn't have to go past the tip, but everyone knew it was there. In summer the tip stank as the rubbish decayed in the heat. It was better in winter when people lit fires there and the smoke was rich and fruity. We parked on the side of the road and tried to hammer the first stake into the ground. It only went in a few inches before it hit rock. We took turns. Each of us thought the other wasn't doing it right, until we had tried for ourselves. As I hit the stake with the mallet and the force reverberated, not into the ground, but back up my arm and shoulder, I knew we were no longer a family. A woman and two boys is not a family. We had no muscle. We had no way of breaking through.

It rained overnight. My mother insisted that we go back and try to erect the signs the next day, as the ground would be softer. With my father gone I had to sit next to my mother in the front seat of the car as she drove. She was wearing Nathan's old raincoat from scouts and a red gingham headscarf over her hair. I told her that it would suit her better if she tied it under her throat like the Queen.

'This way,' I said, as I turned in the seat and knotted it under her chin, 'is more dignified.' I was already a foot taller than her and I was worried someone from school might see us and think she was my girlfriend, instead of my mother. My brother sat in the back of the car while my mother swung at the stake with the mallet. The rain had muddied the surface of the ground, but barely soaked in at all. It was still hard going. It started to drizzle. I held the Lorazepam® High-Potency Benzodiazepine golf umbrella over my mother's head with my arm outstretched so I didn't have to stand too close to her. If anyone drove past and saw us I hoped they would think I was more in the role of caddy than lover.

Increasingly, when I thought about my father, my memories of him were not so much of actual events or incidents, but of the things he left behind. My father had a moustache and one of his eyes was sleepy. The sleepy eye was more noticeable in photographs than in real life. Not many adults have a sleepy eye – or perhaps it's difficult to tell because so many of them wear glasses. There was a framed photograph of my parents on their wedding day next to the telephone in the hall. My mother is wearing a too-big navy suit in the photograph. Her cheeks are uneven and she looks seasick. My father seems happier – his moustache, if not his mouth, is smiling. His eyes are downcast though. He is looking at the most striking thing in the photograph – his massive white wrists. My father told me the story of the photograph one night when he'd been drinking and my mother wouldn't let him in the house. He climbed through my window and spent the night on the floor next to my bed. The story was this: a few months after the date with my mother, my father had another date. This date was with a girl he really liked, a girl he wanted to marry. He paid a friend who worked in a garage to give him the keys to a sports car for the evening so he could take the first rate girl out. Showing off, he took a corner too fast and crashed into a brick wall. The girl was unhurt, but my father broke both of his wrists. Because of this he was wearing plaster casts on his wrists when he married my mother a couple of months later. The casts give my father a serious and masculine appearance in the wedding photograph. The weight of them on his wrists make his arms look heavy, almost burdened, with muscle. And the thickness and hardness of the casts straining at his shirt cuffs is menacing. He doesn't look like a sales clerk, he looks like a boxer.

Underneath the photograph, in the drawer of the hall table, there are three boxes of white biros with blue writing on them – Aldactone® Spironolactone Easy To Swallow Tablets. One afternoon after school I try all of the biros on the back cover of the phone book. Out of fifty-four biros, only seven work.

Because my mother goes on a few dates with one of the real estate agents and it doesn't work out, she has to leave her job. She goes on benefits and is made to do courses. Her course at the local neighbourhood house is called 'Starting Again for the Divorced and Separated'. My mother does her homework in her *My New Life Workbook* in front of the television. When she gets up to go to the toilet during a commercial break I take a look at what she's written. Under *'What motivates me?'* she has answered, *'flowers'*.

My mother asks me and Nathan to go with her to a Parents without Partners picnic. It's at an animal nursery. I can tell that Nathan doesn't mind the sound of it, that he would like to pet the lambs and the rabbits. But I say we are too old, that it's dumb, and by holding Nathan's eye for long enough I get him to agree. My mother goes without us. She meets a man who works on prawn trawlers in the Gulf of Carpentaria. The man has a daughter whom he sees sometimes when he's in town. My mother has a lot of late-night telephone conversations with the man on the prawn trawler. She has to say 'over' when she finishes what she is saying, because he is using a radio telephone. When the prawn season finishes, my mother's new boyfriend moves in with us.

I have become so familiar with the playmates in my father's *Playboy* magazines that they don't work anymore, so I read the articles. In *Playboy* forum, men write in and describe how they meet women in ordinary places; the petrol station, the laundromat or the video library, and they have sex with them against the bowser, the dryers, or on the counter. When this happens a friend of the woman with different coloured hair often arrives unexpectedly and has no hesitation joining in. And if the first woman at the petrol station, the laundromat, or the video library has small breasts, her friend will always have large breasts – or the other way around. After I've read all of the articles I look at the ads and the fashion pages and choose things. I choose Rigs Pants, Lord Jim Bionic Hair Tonic, Manskins jocks, Laredo heeled cowboy boots with a fancy shaft, and Aramis Devin aftershave – the world's first great sporting fragrance for men. I think I hear someone outside, but it's just a pair of dusty boxing gloves that hang from a nail on the back door of the shed. When it's windy the gloves bang into each other. I can no longer remember if the boxing gloves belonged to my father, or if they were in the shed before we came to live here.

Nathan joins the gymnastics team at school and I get a checkout job on Thursday nights and Saturday mornings. Nathan's legs are bowed and he doesn't have any strength in his upper arms. When he does his exercises his shorts ride up and his orange jocks show. The gymnastics teacher says his vaulting technique is poor. He tells me that Nathan doesn't look like he's trying to jump over the horse, more like he's trying to fuck it. He tells me this because I am standing next to my mother in the school quadrangle at open day where we are watching a display of gymnastics. I am wearing my

Coles New World tie and the gymnastics teacher
must think I am my mother's boyfriend. Nathan is
best at the type of gymnastics where he has to
throw a stick or play with a ball – a type of
gymnastics that might have been invented by
puppies. Because Nathan's wrists are weak he
wears special white tape around them. He brings
some of the tape home – he says the gymnastics
teacher gave it to him, but I doubt it. Nathan wears
the tape on his wrists every day during the school
holidays. When the tape gets grubby he puts more
over the top until his wrists are so thick he can't
hold his fork properly. When he's talking he throws
his hands around in the air and watches them. This
is something I've seen my mother do when she has
just changed her nail polish.

By over-ringing the total on a number of
small sales, it is safe to take around five dollars out
of the till at work each week. It's better not to take
an even amount. Four dollars thirty nine is good.
Playboy magazine costs two dollars. I don't buy it
every month. I buy it when the cover looks like it
will go with the covers of my father's magazines
already in the shed.

My mother takes her wedding photograph
out of the frame on the hall table and replaces it
with a picture of herself and her new boyfriend on
a fishing trip. The photograph shows my mother
and Wayne standing on a jetty together, each
holding a fishing line with a white fish dangling
from it. My mother's face is puffy with the strain

of holding the fish aloft. Her lips are open and stretched tight, just like the fishes lips. If it were a group portrait you would have said my mother and the fish were related. My parents' wedding photograph is relegated to a drawer in the hall table where the envelopes and takeaway menus are kept. The photograph rises to the surface every time I search for a piece of paper to take down a message. It is crumpled now and smells of soy sauce.

There is a letter in the latest *Playboy* that I think might be from my father. In the letter a man describes an encounter he has with a woman at a bodybuilding centre. The man describes himself as well built, with a full head of hair and a moustache. He is lifting weights on his own late one night when a beautiful girl comes in to clean the equipment.

The girl is wearing a short pink cleaner's dress which fits poorly across the chest. Because her washing machine has broken down and she is poor and has no change for the laundromat, she is not wearing any underpants. The girl says hello to the man shyly and starts cleaning. The man is sweating heavily – sweat is running off his biceps like he's standing under a waterfall. The man notices that the girl is watching him. He decides to do a few rounds with the punching bag. He calls the girl (she has been bent over rubbing the weight lifting bars with a cloth), and asks her to help him lace up his boxing gloves. As soon as the girl gets close to the man, she is intoxicated by his sweat. She ties the laces of the boxing gloves together so he is her prisoner. She tells the man to sit down on the bench press, then she takes her dress off and rides him like he's a bucking bronco.

The letter is signed, *Hot and Sweaty, Tweed Heads*. I hope that it is my father's letter. I hope the girl in the story is the same girl my father took out on a date when he broke his wrists, and when she finally takes off his boxing gloves and they hold hands, I hope they are not joined by one of her friends with different-coloured hair. I place the magazine on the top of the pile so Nathan will read it too. I hope Nathan will think that our father is happy. I want Nathan to understand that our mother was never going to make things work with our father. She was the wrong girl. And because she was the wrong girl, Nathan and I were the wrong sons. It could never have been any other way.

A Lovely and Terrible Thing

Chris Womersley

WHAT A BURDEN it is to have seen wondrous things, for afterwards the world feels empty of possibility. There used to be a peculiar human majesty in my line of work: the woman with hair so long she could wind it ten times around her waist; old Frankie Block, who could wrestle a horse to the ground; the boy with a fox tail. There was a good reason we referred to ourselves as The Weird Police. Now it's more likely to be a conga-line of Elvis impersonators sponsored by McDonalds. Somewhere along the way the job lost its magic, but perhaps that was just me.

It was dusk when I pulled over to phone my wife. I would be gone for only two nights, but caring for our daughter Therese was gruelling, melancholy work, like tending to a fire perpetually on the verge of going out. More than once I had come home to discover Elaine sitting in the near-dark, weeping with the endlessness of it all, and there was nothing I could do but hold her until she felt better. It took hours, sometimes. At others, all night.

My phone didn't have reception out on the back roads. I trudged into a cold and muddy field with it held foolishly over my head, but it was no use; I would have to call from the motel in Kyneton.

When I returned to the car, the damn thing refused to start. I fished out a torch, popped the bonnet and peered at the engine, but the mass of wires and pipes might as well have been Sanskrit hieroglyphs for all the sense I could make of them. No cars passed. There was not a house in sight. I cursed my decision to take the scenic route. At least on the highway someone might stop and help. On the highway my phone would have reception.

I jiggled a few wires and checked the radiator, but it was no use. By now the horizon was darkening and the wind had turned sharp and bitter. Again I stared at the mute, incomprehensible engine and it occurred to me that a mechanic might have fared better with Therese than any of her medical specialists had over the years. I held my freezing hands over the engine, but the heat it gave off was minimal and diminished noticeably as I stood there.

I was beginning to resign myself to the

prospect of spending the night in the car when a voice startled me. I swung around to see a large man approaching through the gloom. 'G'day,' he said again.

Embarrassed to have been discovered warming myself over a dead engine, I took my hands back and greeted him.

'Everything alright?' he asked.

I gestured to the engine. 'Car's broken down on me. I pulled over to make a phone call and now it won't start.'

The fellow was about my age, dressed in overalls, with a shock of grey hair that flapped about like a bird's broken wing. He stood nodding at the roadside verge and considered me for a moment. 'Want me to take a look?'

'Yes, that would be great. Thanks.' I held out my hand. 'I'm Daniel Shaw, by the way.'

The man grunted and shook my hand, reluctantly, it seemed. 'Dave. They call me Angola 'round here.'

'An*gola*. Like the place?'

He started. 'You've heard of it?'

'Of course.'

He paused. 'Well, I spent a few years there.'

He took my torch, positioned it on the rim of the bonnet where it would provide the best light, and set about poking around inside. After a few minutes he urged me to try the ignition again, which I did, but without any luck.

'Dunno mate,' Angola said, wiping his hands on a rag he produced from a back pocket. 'Reckon she's stuffed for now, though. Where you going?'

'Kyneton. How far is that?'

Again he looked at me as if puzzled to find me there at all. By now it was almost dark. The only light was that of the torch which, at that moment, splashed its light across the right half of his face. I imagined us from a distance – two men, strangers to each other, on a lonely road – and felt a jolt of fear.

'Too far to walk,' he said at last above a roar of sudden wind. He undid the bracket supporting the upraised bonnet, grabbed the torch and let the bonnet fall. 'But you can stay the night at my place, if you like.'

'I need to be there by 2pm tomorrow afternoon. There's something I have to verify. I work for Ripley's Believe it or Not, and there's supposed to be a parrot that can count to 150. I have to check it's true. We might use it in the next annual.'

That piqued his interest. It usually did. Angola sauntered closer and looked me over. 'You work for Ripley's? Like the TV show? Ha. You musta seen some pretty weird things.'

I laughed. The world's most-tattooed man, the girl with 18 fingers, the ultra-marathon runners. He didn't know the half of it.

With his thumb he indicated the field beside the road, beyond which, presumably, he lived. 'My daughter has a pretty special trick, actually. Maybe

you should come and see her? Put her in your big
old book.'

He said this in a mildly lascivious manner I
didn't care for but, as usual, that word pricked my
heart, deflating it ever further. *Daughter.* I thought
again of poor Elaine, poor Therese; my silent,
waiting family. I hoped my wife had at least turned
on the lights before pouring her first Scotch.

'You got kids?' Angola asked me, handing
back the torch.

'Yes, I have a daughter, too, as a matter of fact.'

He grinned. 'Then you know what a lovely
and terrible thing it is.'

It was an incongruous and curiously poetic
description, particularly coming from his gap-
toothed mouth. I nodded. For a moment I could
not speak. I looked off into the bleak distance, then
at this man, and there was something about the sad
shake of his head and the way his hair flapped
about on his scalp that filled me with unreasonable
warmth. A decent man out here in the country,
with mud on his boots and the grease of a stranger's
car on his hands.

For reasons best known only to the darker
parts of myself, I felt immense shame about
Therese, and rarely told anyone of my troubles; I
had colleagues, for instance, who were completely
unaware of her existence. But, for some reason, out
on this road, I felt compelled to tell this man what
had happened to her.

I coughed into my fist. 'But my daughter is

– she was in an accident. Eight years ago. She cycled onto the road when she was eleven and got hit by a car. She lost the use of her legs and became brain damaged. We don't even know if she knows who we are – my wife and I, I mean. They say – the *experts*, that is – to hope for a miracle, that she might recover some of her movement and coordination. It has happened before, you know. Small breakthroughs, they say. Keep an eye out for small breakthroughs, whatever they might be.' I could have bored the poor fellow with talk of trauma and lobes and the ripple effect, but instead I tapped my head with my index finger. 'We don't really know what goes on in there.'

It was at this point that people usually said something consoling, along the lines of *I'm sure she'll come good one of these days*, but the man called Angola merely stared at me, listening, until I said all I had to say. And it was perhaps for this kindness that I enquired after the 'trick' of his daughter's. Normally I would not follow up on every stranger's claim – for we all believed our children to be possessed of special talents, even those of us whose faith has been worn so thin – but I felt I owed him this small courtesy.

Angola waved my polite query away. 'Oh,' he said. 'You'd never believe me.'

'I've heard some pretty wild stories, you know.'

He looked at me for a long time, as if attempting to peer into my soul. It was unsettling.

I saw now – by what light I couldn't say, for the sun had well and truly set – that his face was pitted with acne scars and that his left earlobe was malformed. But there, by the road, he told me something so bizarre, and in such a strange manner – looking from side to side, shrugging, mumbling – that I had no choice but to believe him.

I carried the torch as we squelched across a field and ducked between the barbed wire of several fences. I asked him about Africa, but he was reluctant to disclose his reasons for being there and became curiously sullen, saying merely that it was a terrible place and that he hadn't deserved to be there at all.

It was only when we saw the lights of his small house in the distance that I realised, and stopped. 'Your name,' I said, trying to keep the panic from my voice. 'It's not for the country is it?'

My companion paused and wiped his meaty paw beneath his nose.

It was freezing. My shoes were sticky with mud. 'It's for the prison, isn't it? In America.' I recalled an entry from the 1972 Ripley's annual; an inmate who – although he had never left the state of Louisiana – built a precise scale model of central Paris from toothpicks, complete with street signs and roadside markets, tiny apples and pears.

'Course it is,' he growled, and continued walking.

I stared after him until I could barely make

him out in the darkness. I pondered my options, which were few. After a minute, I staggered after him.

It was a decision I have come to regret.

Angola's house was large, but cluttered with thick-legged furniture, piles of toys and the detritus of domestic activity: mounds of knitting, fishing bags, a cricket set. Angola's wife Carol, elbow-deep in dishwater, seemed perplexed to see me in her house but shook my hand with her own sudsy one and offered me a beer. A teenage boy appeared and grunted at his father before skulking off. I peered around for the daughter about whom I had heard such amazing things, but there was no sign of her. Another son materialised, dutifully shook my hand and vanished. The television blared and I recognised the dopey voice-overs of *Australia's Funniest Home Videos*. The sons laughed themselves stupid at something. *I think I'll just take a walk up here on the icy roof...* Angola and his wife bickered good-naturedly about an unpaid bill. *Boinggg.*

With their permission, I phoned Elaine from the dim, unheated study at the rear of the house. The window sills were lined with children's sporting trophies. Football, cricket, tennis. *Best and Fairest. Under 12 Champion.* The small desk was covered with bank statements, shopping catalogues, letters from a local school.

Elaine sounded harried – but not drunk, at least. Her French-accented voice was damp with unshed tears. Not for the first time I felt I might have been starring unwittingly in some mournful, European film. She had had a bad day of it: a tradesman had tracked mud into the house and then been unable to fix a pipe we had been waiting on for two weeks; Therese had to be changed three times.

'But she did a funny thing, Dan. You won't believe this but I went in this afternoon, she was in the sunroom – you know how she loves to stare at the birds at the feeder – and I swear she reached out to stroke my hair as I leaned over her.'

I paused to take this in. I heard our fridge humming in the background. 'Are you sure?'

'Yes.'

'She stroked your *hair*?'

'Yes.'

This could be a breakthrough. I leaned forward, elbows on the desk. 'For how long?'

'Well. A few seconds.'

'It could be something, though, couldn't it?'

'Sure. Yeah.'

'It wasn't just a –'

'Dan. I'm sure.'

Pinned to the wall above the desk where I sat was a child's drawing of a dog. Bulbous shapes conjoined by stick-like limbs, a scribble of blue cloud. I imagined Therese in her low bed staring at the ceiling where I had stuck luminous stars; her implacable face, her shining eyes. She might have contained entire oceans, shipwrecked galleons, dragons, concertos. I loved my daughter more when I was away from her; her actual presence only highlighted my inability to help her. My beery breath bounced back at me from the plastic receiver, and for the thousandth time since her accident I was flooded with sudden, acute disappointment at how I had so quickly reached the limits of my love.

I told Elaine I would be back the day after tomorrow at the latest, depending how long it took to get the car repaired.

'Dan?'

'Yes.'

'Do you promise?'

She often asked me that. 'Yes,' I said.

Returning to the lounge room, I passed a carpeted hallway I hadn't noticed earlier. Pop music drifted through a part-open door at the other end and a long matchstick of light fell on the swirling carpet. This must be the daughter's bedroom. I paused to listen, as if the music might offer a clue. *I should be so lucky, lucky, lucky, lucky.* Kylie Minogue. Hysterical laughter from the lounge-room, Angola asking his sons something. I shuffled down the hall towards the daughter's room. She was singing along to the music in a low voice. Despite myself, I sensed the thrill of discovering something truly incredible. What if her father had been telling the truth? I crept closer, almost holding my breath.

'You right, mate?'

I swivelled around to see Angola standing at the other end of the corridor. Although he was in silhouette, I could tell he was glaring at me. 'Yes, I was just—'

'That's Chloe's room.'

'Oh. I was, ah, looking for the bathroom.'

It was clear he didn't believe me. He wiped the back of his hand under his nose, then pointed the way I had come. 'That way. And dinner's ready.'

In any case, I didn't have long to wait before seeing the daughter. When I returned from the bathroom, the family was gathered at the dinner table and looked up expectantly at my entrance. The daughter, Chloe, was seated opposite me. She looked ordinary enough, but I couldn't help inspecting her whenever the opportunity arose.

Dinner was roast lamb with mint sauce and vegetables. Everyone talked at once. The boys bickered and thumped each other. Carol lit up a cigarette at the table as soon as she had eaten. Angola talked on his mobile phone for several minutes. The television raved away in the background. It was disconcerting to be at such a rowdy family dinner, but gradually, with the help of a few beers, I began to enjoy myself. *So*, I thought, *this is family life*.

Angola had cooled towards me, but I regaled the gathering with tales from my years as a verifier for Ripley's. Soon they were all laughing and wide-eyed, gasping in astonishment at South

Pacific cargo cults, at the man who dived into buckets of water from great heights, the parachutist who shaved and smoked a cigarette in the time it took to float back to earth.

Angola picked something from his teeth. 'And do people make, you know, *money* out of these things?'

'Sure,' I said. 'Sometimes.'

At this, Angola's wife uttered a curious sound. I could restrain myself no longer and turned to the girl Chloe, who had been quiet the entire meal. 'So. Your father tells me that you have quite an unusual talent yourself? Would you like to show me what you can do?'

The family fell silent. Then Carol put her head in her hands. 'Jesus, Dave. I *knew it*. You told him didn't you? I knew it…'

Angola started to protest, but his justifications were trumped by the only words I heard Chloe speak. 'No,' she piped, 'that's my sister Emily. She's in the shed.'

The shed was really a stable about 100 metres from the house. A wind buffeted us as we made our way across the yard with a torch. I was anxious. Many years ago I met a woman who claimed to have a portion of Hitler's jawbone – complete with some piece of paperwork or other that verified it – but from the moment I stepped into her stinking, ramshackle entrance hall I knew she was just a lonely madwoman with a house full of junk. That I fell for it has long been a source of embarrassment for me, but in my business one needed to check all reasonable leads. Would this perhaps be the same? Or even worse?

Angola unbolted the massive door and swung it open. The stable was dimly lit. Pausing on the threshold, I could smell wet hay and the sweat of animals. I knew the rest of the family were standing at the kitchen window, watching to see what I, a stranger, would make of their daughter. After the other daughter Chloe had spoken up at the dinner table, there had been a heated discussion of money, of fame and reality TV that I did my best to dampen while still allowing them enough enthusiasm to show me their curious prize.

I stepped inside. Angola followed and closed the door behind me. Something stirred in a far corner, I heard a clank of chain. Angola brushed past me and went to another door on the other side of the stable. He paused with his hand on the wooden knob. 'You ready?'

I nodded. By this time my heart was hammering. The miraculous has a smell, and this Godforsaken place was ripe with it. Angola opened the door and went in. Another rustle of chain, the swish of straw. Murmured words, kindly words. He beckoned me over. 'Don't be afraid,' he said, then to his daughter: 'This is Mr Shaw, love.'

I said hello and drifted into the room, which

was spacious, decorated like any 14-year-old girl's room: posters of pop stars, family photographs, drawings of horses. The girl, Emily was sitting on a low bed placed along one wall. She was slight, pretty, with long brown hair and large eyes. She looked momentarily startled, but quickly recovered, said good evening and smiled. It was clear we had interrupted her reading a book; it was placed face-down on the bed next to her. Then I saw the iron hoop around her ankle and the short chain attached at the other end to the bed frame. Emily noticed me staring at it and shrugged. Angola seemed nervous and asked her if she might show me her trick.

'It's not a trick, Pa,' she admonished.

Angola unlocked the iron hoop. 'Well. You know what I mean, love.'

Emily rolled her eyes.

Angola dropped the key to her bolt into his coat pocket and stepped back. He offered me an apologetic smile. 'Teenagers, eh?'

Emily swung around until both legs hung over the edge of her bed. Angola and I waited by the door. Horses moved around nervously in their stalls nearby.

'Are you sure, Pa?'

Angola nodded.

'But you said that –'

'Emily. This man might be able to help us.'

'OK.'

And after a few minutes, it happened, as

Angola had said it would. Almost imperceptibly, Emily began to levitate from the bed with no apparent exertion. The space between the hem of her dress and the rumpled bed expanded. Her face wore the beatific expression of one rapt in an interior activity like, say, listening to a favourite piece of music or contemplating a scene of sublime beauty. The entire thing happened in silence. When at last I could speak, I asked Angola how long she had been doing this.

'Oh, only two months or so. Not long.' It was clear that, behind his anxiety over what was happening to his daughter, he was very proud.

Meanwhile, Emily rose higher and higher. After several minutes, she put out a hand to prevent her head bumping against the high ceiling. Gently she shoved herself off, whereupon she drifted down and across the room before again floating to the ceiling. Finally, Angola took a length of rope, flung up it to his daughter and hauled her down to the floor, as one might a boat to a pier.

He secured Emily to her bed with the iron bolt. They exchanged tender words. He thanked her, kissed her on the forehead. We left the barn. Then he turned to me with an avaricious gleam in his eye, and I knew instantly what I had to do.

In the middle of the night, when I was certain the family was asleep, I eased the ring of keys from the hook by the kitchen door and crept out of the house.

Emily didn't seem surprised to see me standing in her room. I sensed her looking at me as soon as I unlocked her door, but she said nothing, uttered not a sound. It was so quiet out there in the country I could hear her breathing in the gloom. I crouched by her bed and told her not to be afraid and she nodded as if she had known all along – known even before I did – what I intended to do. Some girls were like that. I unlocked the iron clasp from her bony ankle, gave her a moment to put a robe over her pyjamas, then lifted her from the bed and carried her outside.

My shoes crunched on the gravel driveway. I registered the familiar pleasing sensation of a girl's warm and trusting breath on my neck, a cheek bumping against my shoulder. I had intended to carry her far beyond the edge of the property, but she was heavier than I anticipated – or I older and wearier – and I was compelled to put her down in the driveway seventy or so metres from the house. The girl uttered a startled laugh, wobbled, then grabbed my sleeve as if momentarily unbalanced on a beam.

I held her by her wrist and we stood there for several seconds staring at each other in silence.

'I'm scared,' she whispered.

'I know. But there is no need to be.'

The moon was high and full. By its light I saw the silvery outline of her jaw, tendrils of her hair waving in the breeze. Experimentally, I loosened my grip on her wrist and we stood there in the driveway, the girl and I, for a few seconds longer until she, too, let go of my sleeve.

I sensed animals moving around us in the darkness, the soft and furry blink of their eyes. Emily smoothed her knotty hair and looked around. For a second I feared she would run or cry out for help but, instead, she looked at me and smiled. 'Good-bye,' she said.

Gradually, she rose into the air as she had done several hours earlier and the sight of it thrilled me anew. Her knobbly knees floated past my face and I realised I was weeping. She stifled a giggle with a hand across her mouth, then relaxed and held out her arms and it seemed to me that she was not rising so much as the earth on which I stood was falling away beneath her feet. She waved. By the time lights came on in the house and I heard angry voices, the girl was already out of reach, floating above a nearby stand of gum trees.

Angola and his family ran up behind me with mouths full of oaths, but instead of escaping, as I should have done, I closed my eyes to better imagine the world from the girl's new height. I wondered if she saw trees in the distance, the yellow gravel of a driveway. Did she hear her father crying out and sense the stars close at hand, the vast and ancient universe into which she was being drawn? Far below, did she make out a man beating another man over and over with his fists, and hear a dog yapping at the commotion? People clawing at each other, throwing up their hands, shrieking?

Finally, when her family below fell silent and looked skyward, each of their faces glowed strangely and were so small they might have been coins on a road as, free at last, she disappeared from sight.

The Authors

Lucy Caldwell was born in Belfast in 1981 and lives in London. She read English at Queen's College, Cambridge and is a graduate of Goldsmith's MA in Creative & Life Writing. She has published two novels, *Where They Were Missed* (2006) and *The Meeting Point* (2011), and her third, *All the Beggars Riding,* will be published in January 2013. *The Meeting Point* featured on BBC Radio 4's *Book at Bedtime* and was awarded the 2011 Dylan Thomas Prize.

She is also a playwright whose stage plays (*Leaves, Guardians, Notes to Future Self*) and radio dramas (*Girl from Mars, Avenues of Eternal Peace, Witch Week*) have won numerous awards including the George Divine Award and the Imison Award. In 2011, Lucy was awarded the prestigious Rooney Prize for Irish Literature for her body of work to date.

M.J. Hyland's first novel, *How the Light Gets In* (2003), was shortlisted for the Commonwealth Writers' Prize. Her second, *Carry me Down* (2006), won the Hawthornden and Encore Prizes in 2007 and was shortlisted for the Man Booker Prize. Her third novel, *This is How*, was longlisted for both the

Orange Prize and the International IMPAC Prize.

Her short fiction has been published frequently in *Zoetrope:All-Story*, *Blackbook Magazine* (USA) and *Best Australian Short Stories,* whilst her journalism regularly features in publications including the *London Review of Books*, *Irish Independent* and the *Guardian*.

Before her first novel was published, she worked as a commercial lawyer for seven years and lectured in criminal law. She is currently a lecturer in Creative Writing at the Centre for New Writing at the University of Manchester.

Deborah Levy is a novelist and a playwright and lives in London. She trained at the Dartington College of Arts and was a Fellow in Creative Arts at Trinity College, Cambridge from 1989 to1991. Her novels include *Swimming Home* (2012), *Beautiful Mutants*, *Swallowing Geography*, *The Unloved* and *Billy and Girl*. She has also published several anthologies of short stories, including *Ophelia and the Great Idea* and *Pillow Talk in Europe and Other Places*.

Deborah has written for the Royal Shakespeare Company and her plays are performed all over the world. In 2001, she was awarded a Lannan Literary Fellowship in the US and was a Fellow in Creative and Performing Arts at The Royal College of Art from 2006-2009.

Krys Lee was born in Seoul, South Korea, and was raised in California and Washington. She moved to study in the United States and England. She was a finalist for Best New American Voices and received a special mention in the 2012 Pushcart Prize XXXVI. Krys is the author of the novel *Drifting House* (2012) and her other work has appeared in the *Kenyon Review*, *Narrative Magazine*, *Granta* (New Voices), *California Quarterly*, *Asia Weekly*, the *Guardian*, the *New Statesman*, and *Condé Nast Traveller*. She divides her time between South Korea and the United States.

Adam Ross was born and raised in New York City and now lives in Nashville with his wife and two daughters. He has an MA from Hollins University and an MFA from Washington University in Creative Writing. His debut novel, *Mr. Peanut*, a 2010 *New York Times* Notable Book, was also named one of the best books of the year by *The New Yorker*, *The Philadelphia Inquirer*, *The New Republic*, and *The Economist* and will be published in sixteen countries. *Ladies and Gentlemen*, his short story collection, was included in *Kirkus Reviews* Best Books of 2011. His journalism has been published in *The New York Times* Book Review, *The Daily Beast*, *The Wall Street Journal* , *GQ*, *The Nashville Scene* and *Poets & Writers*. His fiction has appeared in *The Carolina Quarterly* and *Five Chapters*.

Chris Womersley's debut novel, *The Low Road*, won the Ned Kelly Award for Best First Fiction. His second novel, *Bereft*, won the Australian Book Industry Award for Literary Fiction and the Indie Award for Fiction, and was shortlisted for the Miles Franklin Literary Award, *The Age* fiction prize and the Australian Literature Society Gold Medal, as well as being longlisted for the IMPAC Dublin Award 2011. His short story, 'Possibility of Water', won the Josephine Ulrick Literature Award in 2007. Chris is a journalist by training and his fiction and reviews have appeared in *Granta*, *The Best Australian Stories* in 2006, 2010 and 2011, *Griffith Review*, *Meanjin* and *The Age*. He lives in Sydney.

Miroslav Penkov was born in 1982 and raised in Bulgaria. In 2001, he moved to America to study for a bachelor's degree in Psychology and an MFA in Creative Writing from the University of Arkansas. His stories have appeared, among other places, in *The Southern Review*, *The Sunday Times*, *The Best American Short Stories 2008* (edited by Salman Rushdie) and the *PEN/O. Henry Prize Stories 2012*. He is the author of *East of the West: A Country in Stories* (2011), the title story of which appears in this collection. He is an Assistant Professor of Creative Writing at the University of North Texas and is currently a fiction editor for *American Literary Review*.

Julian Gough was born in London and grew up in Ireland. He now lives in Berlin. He won the BBC National Short Story Prize in 2007 with 'The Orphan and the Mob', which later became the prologue for *Jude: Level 1*, a novel shortlisted for the 2008 Wodehouse Prize for Comic Fiction. Julian's first novel, *Juno and Juliet*, was published in 2001, followed by *Jude in Ireland* in 2007. *Jude in London*, his most recent novel, was published in 2011 and was shortlisted for the Bollinger Everyman Wodehouse Prize. In 2010, Salmon Poetry released his first poetry collection, *Free Sex Chocolate*.

Julian Gough has also written columns and opinion pieces for various newspapers and magazines, including the *Guardian*, *Prospect Magazine* and *A Public Space*.

Carrie Tiffany was born in West Yorkshire and grew up in Western Australia. She spent her early 20s working as a park ranger in Central Australia and now lives in Melbourne where she works as an agricultural journalist. Carrie completed a Masters Degree in Creative Writing at RMIT University in Melbourne.

Her first novel, *Everyman's Rules for Scientific Living*, was shortlisted for the Miles Franklin Literary Award, the Victorian Premier's Literary Award, the Orange Prize for Fiction, the Commonwealth Writer's Prize and the Guardian First Book Award, and was the winner of the

Western Australian Premier's Fiction Prize. Her second novel, *Mateship with Birds* was published in 2012.

Henrietta Rose-Innes is a South African writer based in Cape Town. Her novel *Nineveh* (2011) has been shortlisted for the 2012 South African Sunday Times Fiction Prize and won the Caine Prize for African Writing in 2008. She has also written a short-story collection, *Homing* (2010), and two other novels: *Shark's Egg* (2000) and *The Rock Alphabet* (2004). She was awarded the South African PEN Literary Award in 2007 and her story 'Falling' was a runner-up in the 2010 Willesden Herald short story prize. Her short stories have appeared in various publications, including *Granta*, *AGNI* and *The Best American Nonrequired Reading 2011*.

She was a Fellow in Literature at the Akademie Schloss Solitude, Stuttgart (2007-8) and has held various international residencies. Henrietta studied archaeology and completed an MA at the University of Cape Town's Centre for Creative Writing under JM Coetzee in 1999. She has worked in publishing and is currently Donald Gordon Creative Arts Fellow at the Gordon Institute for Performing and Creative Arts (GIPCA), University of Cape Town.